Dear Parent:

Psst . . . you're looking at the Super Secret Weapon of Reading. It's called comics.

STEP INTO READING® COMIC READERS are a perfect step in learning to read. They provide visual cues to the meaning of words and helpfully break out short pieces of dialogue into speech balloons.

Here are some terms commonly associated with comics:
PANEL: A section of a comic with a box drawn around it.
CAPTION: Narration that helps set the scene.
SPEECH BALLOON: A bubble containing dialogue.
GUTTER: The space between panels.

Tips for reading comics with your child:

• Have your child read the speech balloons while you read the captions.
• Ask your child: What is a character feeling? How can you tell?
• Have your child draw a comic showing what happens after the book is finished.

STEP INTO READING® COMIC READERS are designed to engage and to provide an empowering reading experience. They are also fun. The best-kept secret of comics is that they create lifelong readers. *And that will make you the real hero of the story!*

Jenn — *M.Holm*

Jennifer L. Holm and Matthew Holm
Co-creators of the Babymouse and Squish series

For my loves—Danny, Kate, and Jane
—D.M.

For my mom, Anita,
whose constant warmth and support
I could not repay, but I'll try anyway
—G.W.

Text copyright © 2022 by Diana Murray
Cover art and interior illustrations copyright © 2022 by Gal Weizman

All rights reserved. Published in the United States by Random House Children's Books, a division of Penguin Random House LLC, New York.

Step into Reading, Random House, and the Random House colophon are registered trademarks of Penguin Random House LLC.

Visit us on the Web!
StepIntoReading.com
rhcbooks.com

Educators and librarians, for a variety of teaching tools, visit us at RHTeachersLibrarians.com

Library of Congress Cataloging-in-Publication Data is available upon request.
ISBN 978-0-593-48845-4 (trade) — ISBN 978-0-593-48846-1 (lib. bdg.) —
ISBN 978-0-593-48847-8 (ebook)

Printed in the United States of America
10 9 8 7 6 5 4 3 2 1

This book has been officially leveled by using the F&P Text Level Gradient™ Leveling System.

A COMIC READER

STEP INTO READING®

STEP 1

Love STINKS!

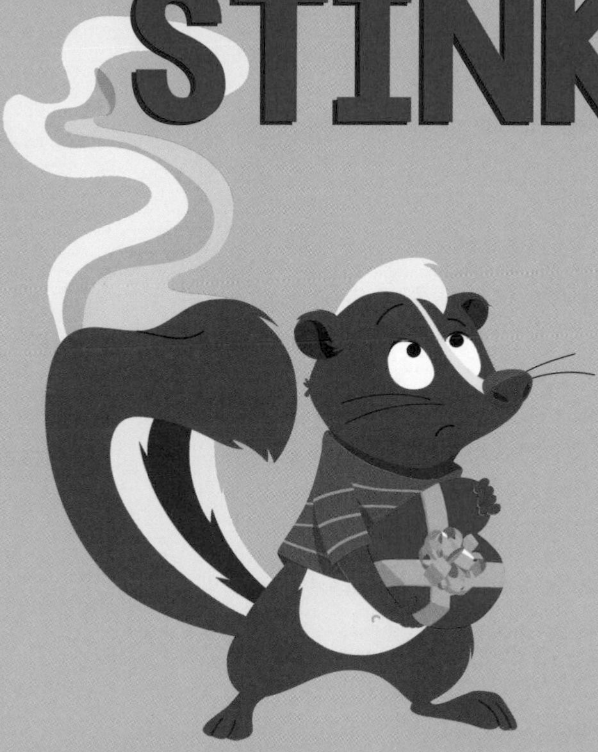

by Diana Murray

illustrated by Gal Weizman

Random House New York

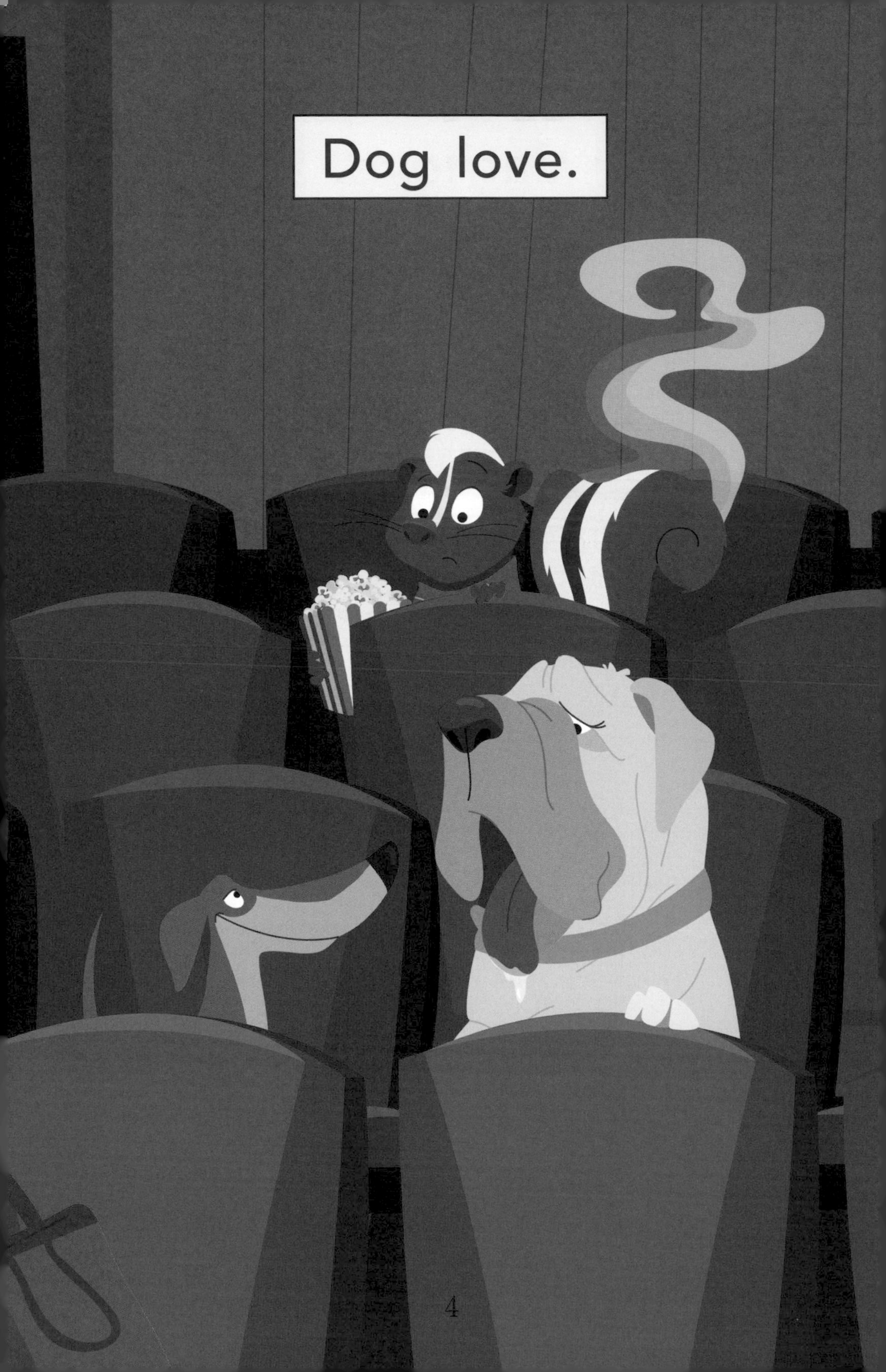

Dog love.

Cat love.

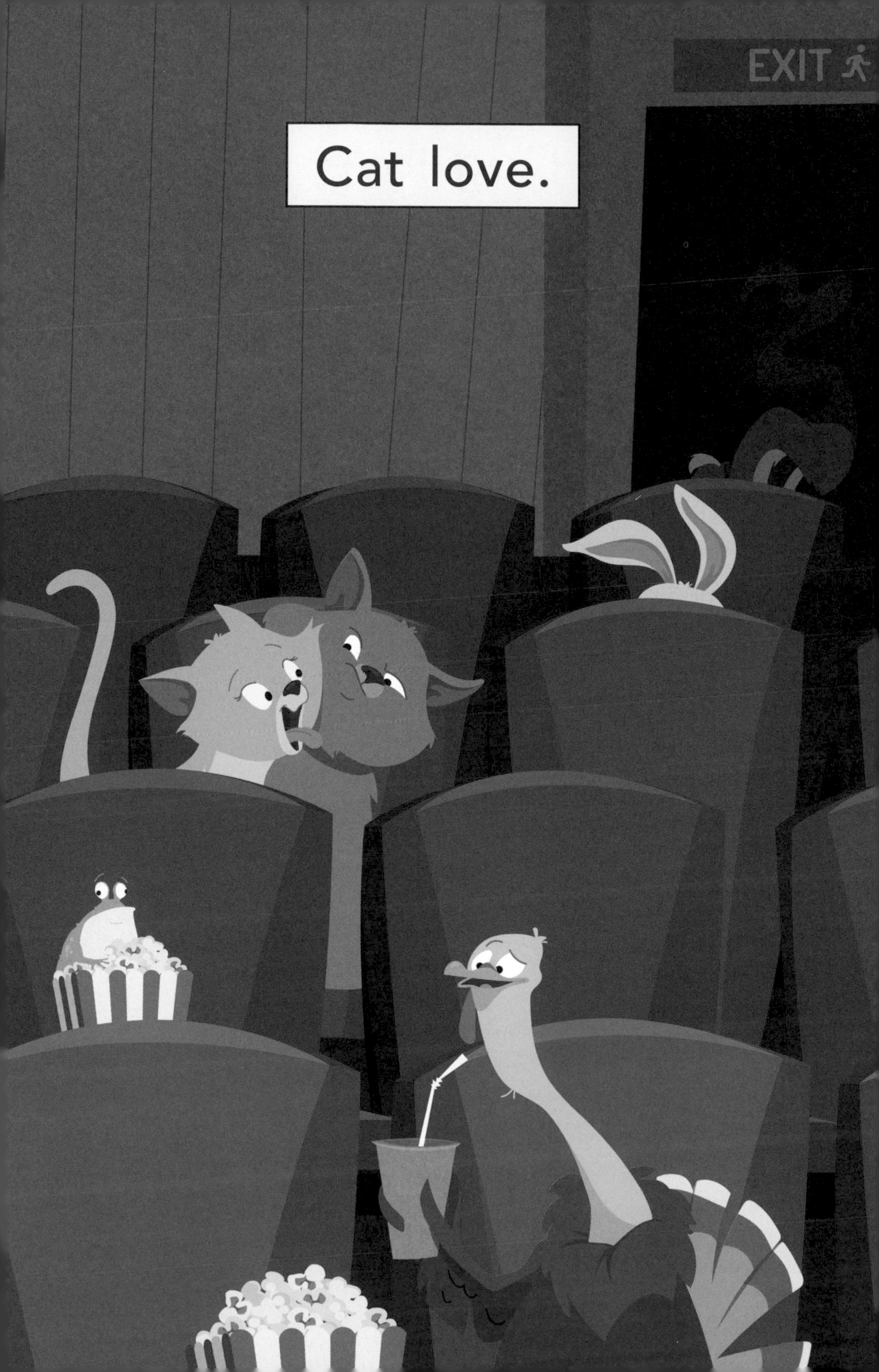
EXIT

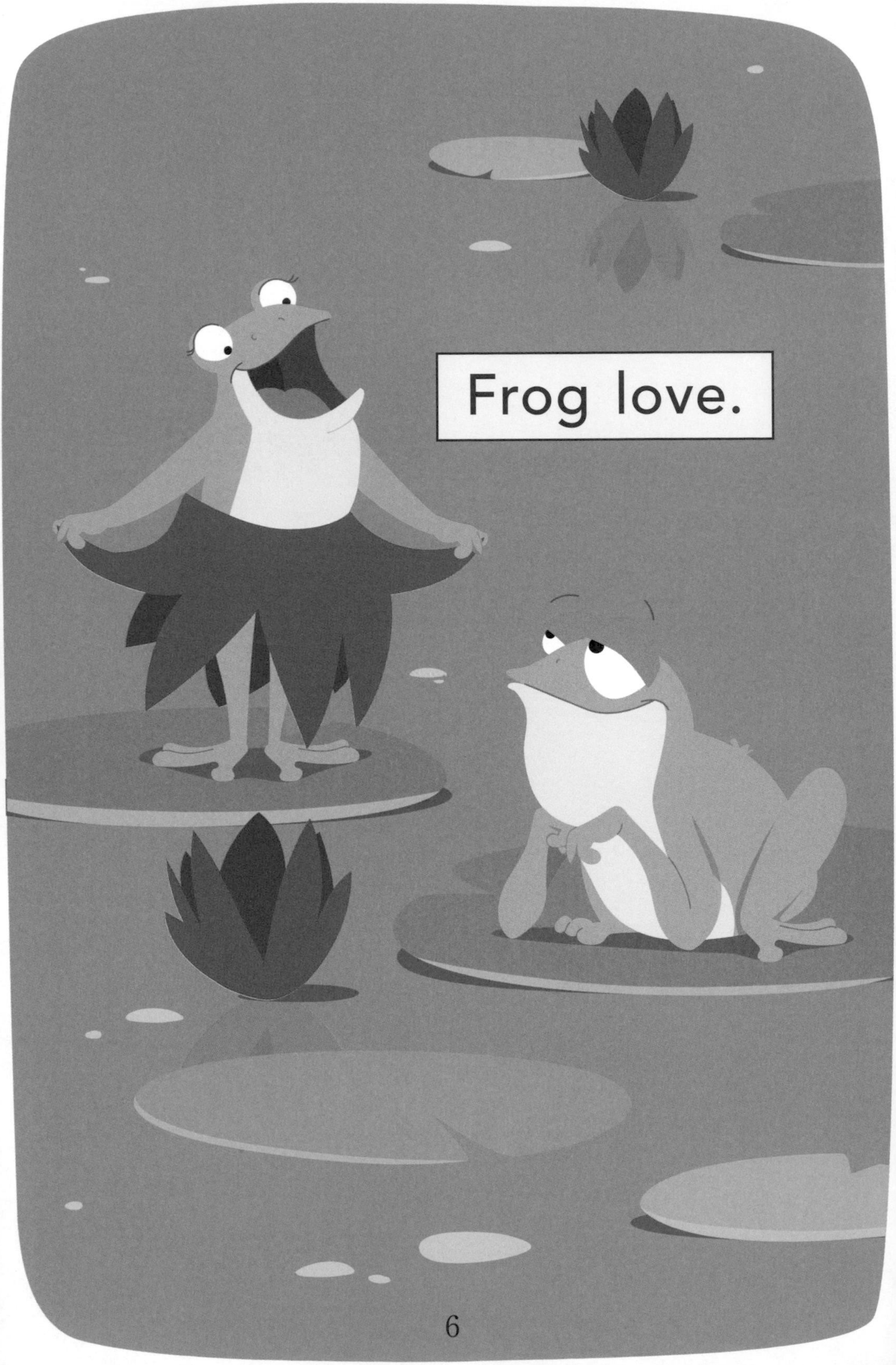

Frog love.

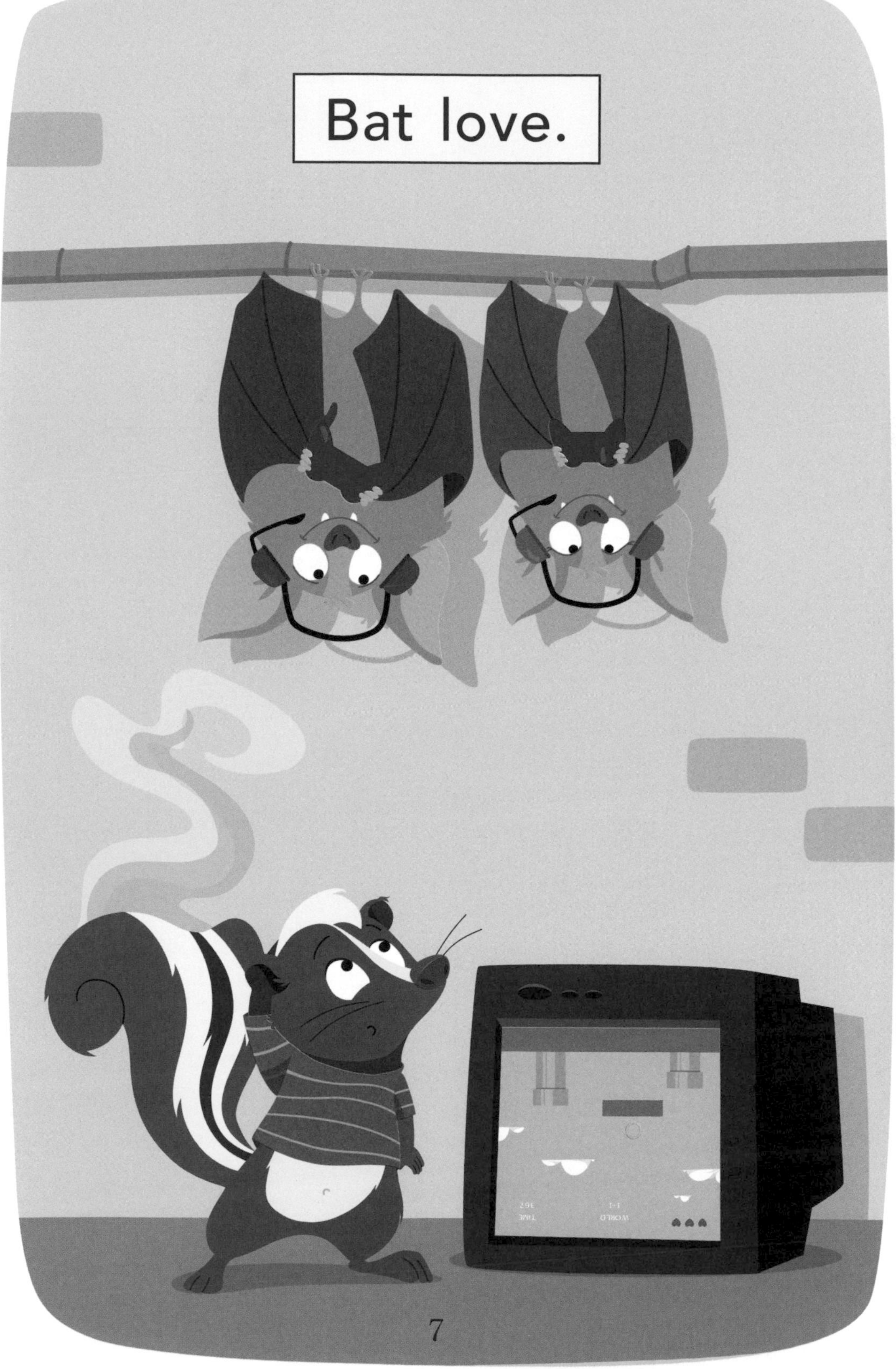
Bat love.

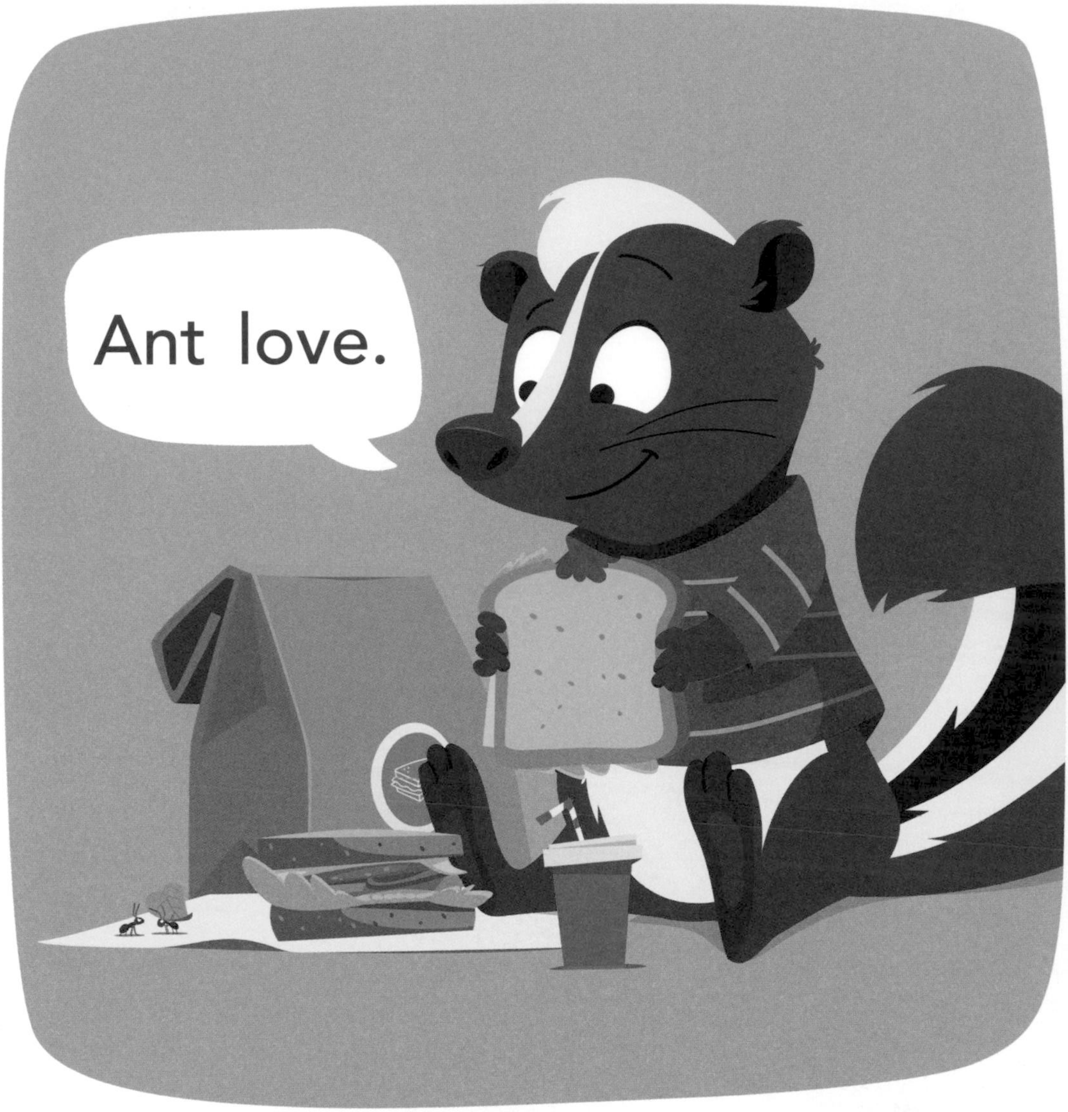
Ant love.

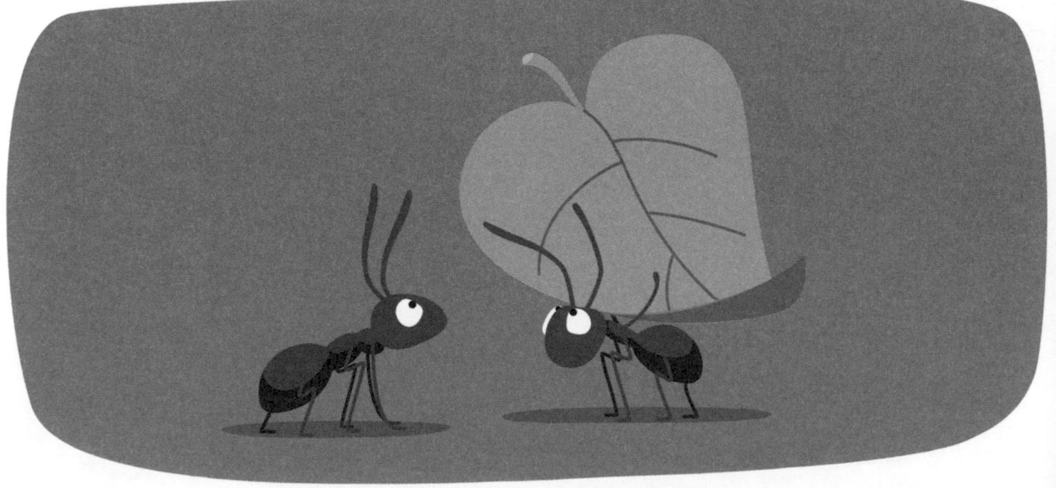

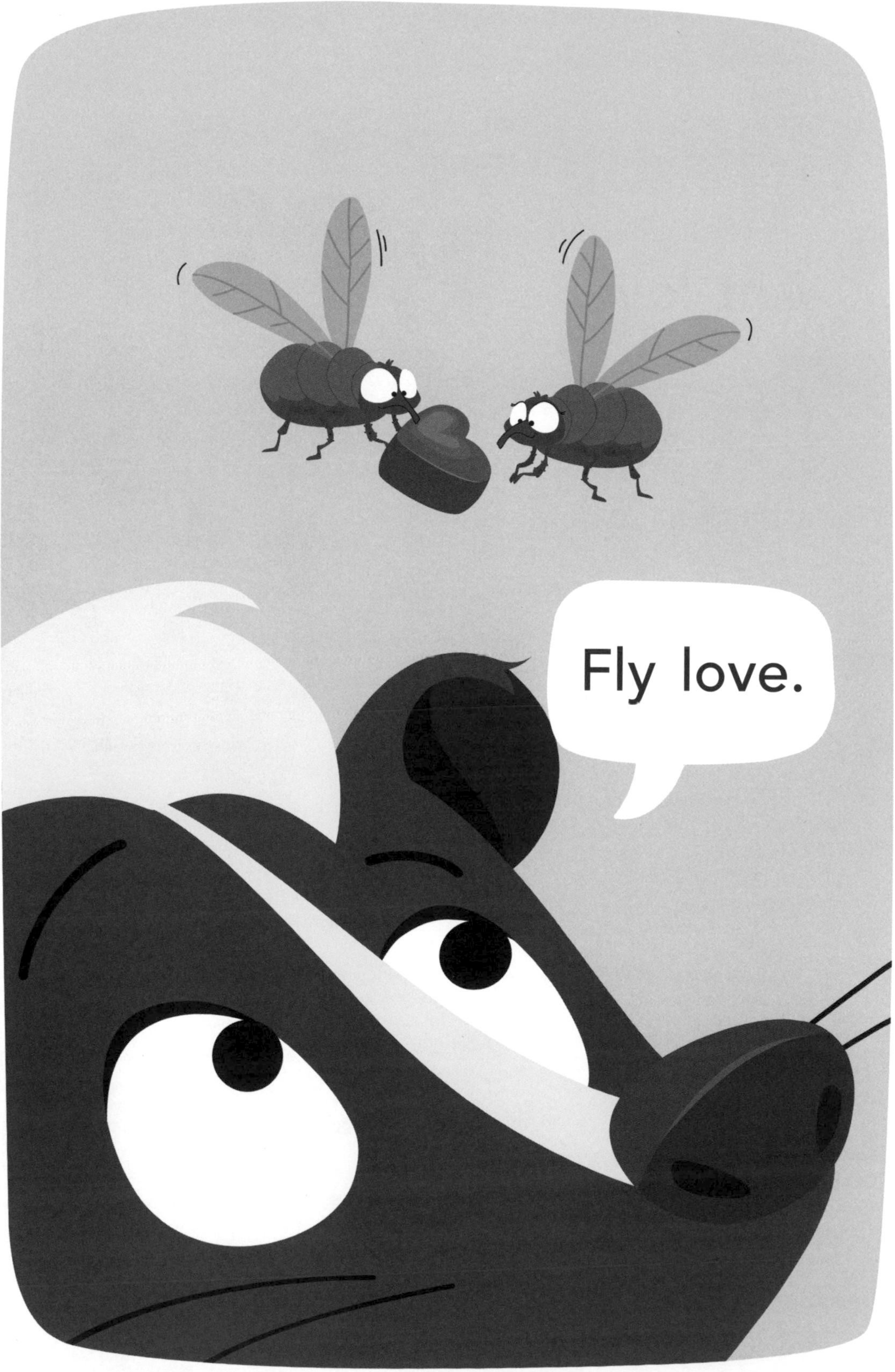
Fly love.

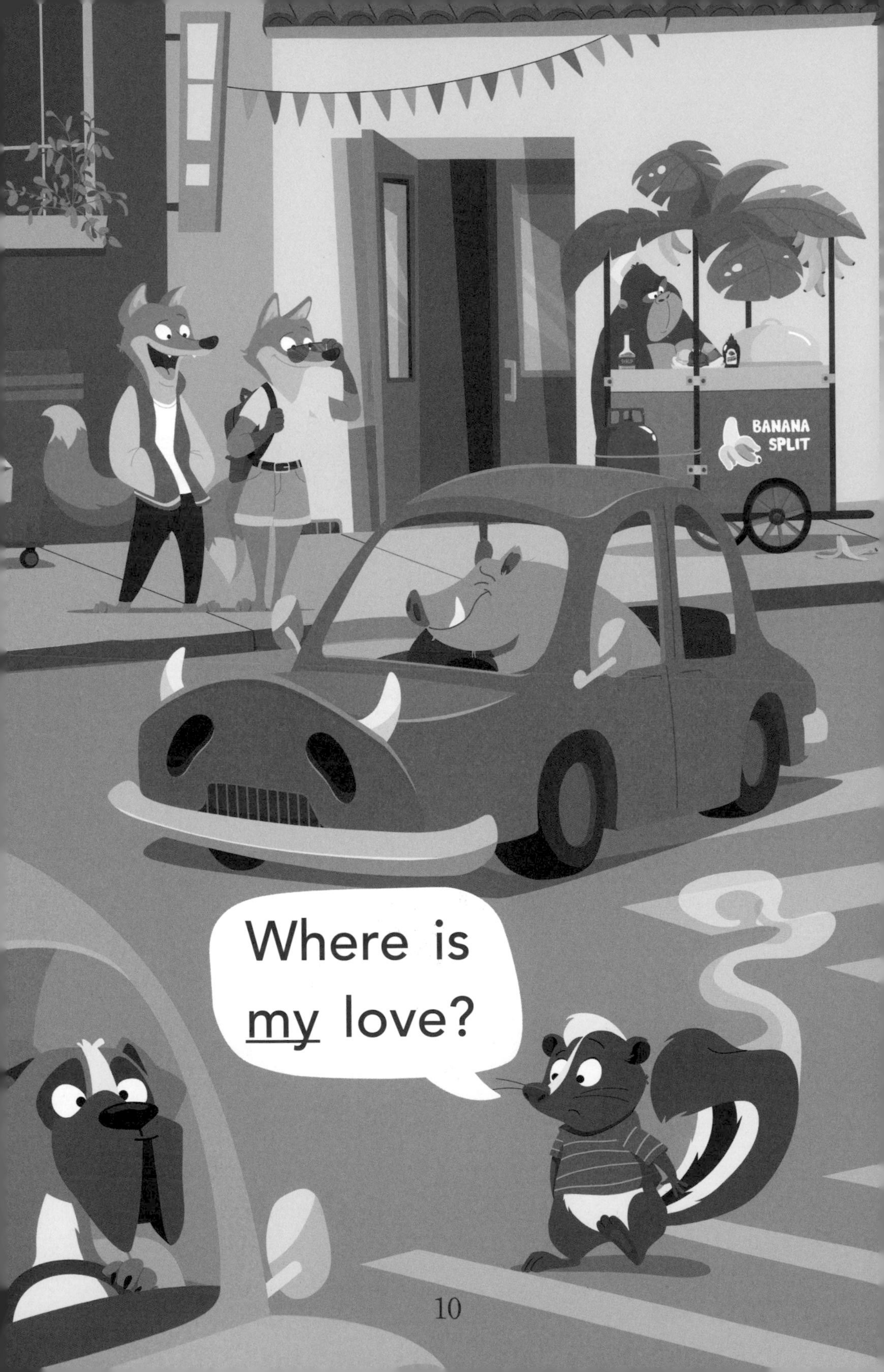
BANANA SPLIT
Where is my love?

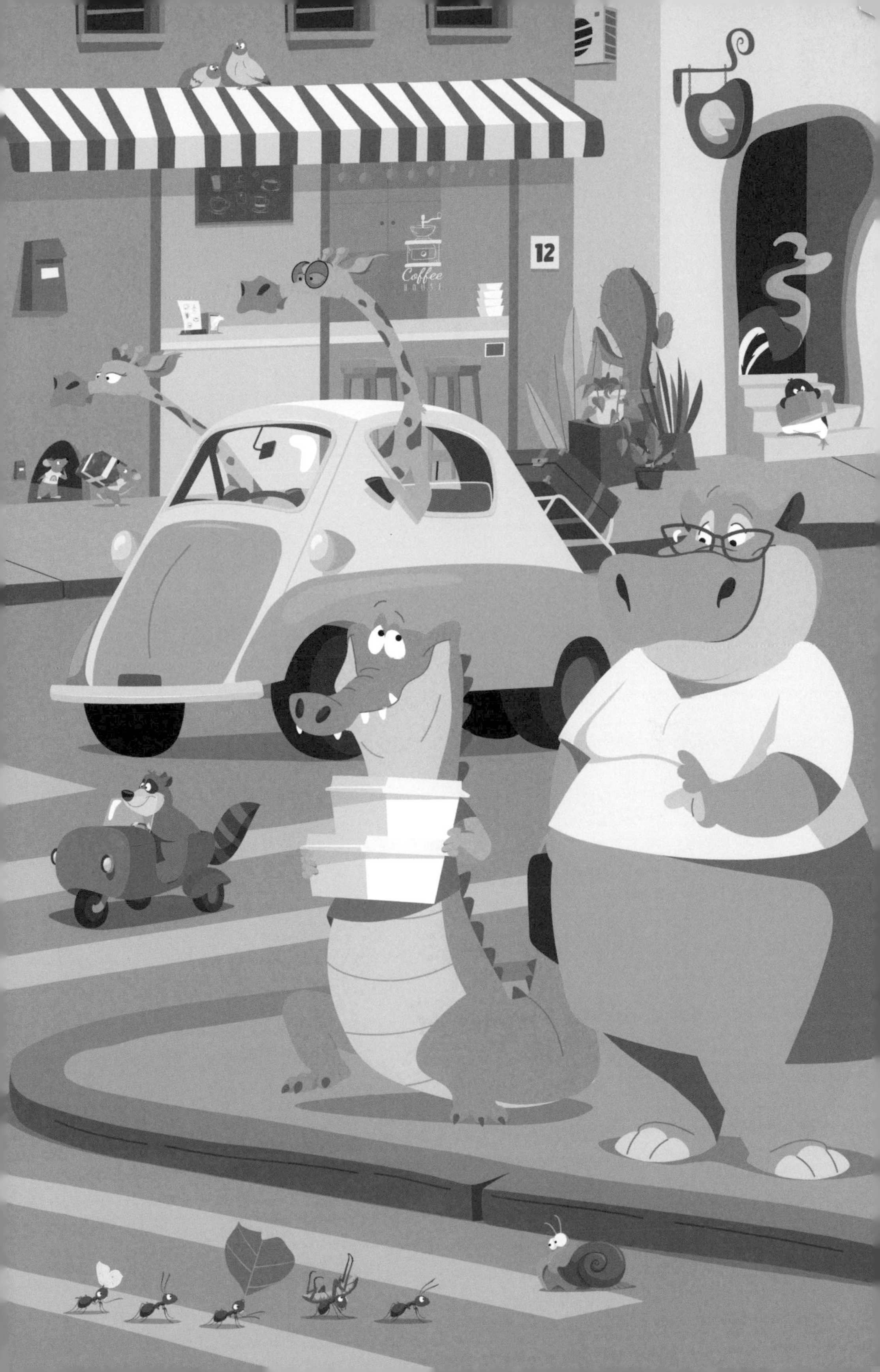
12
Coffee
HOUSE

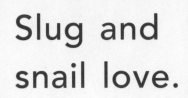

Slug and
snail love.

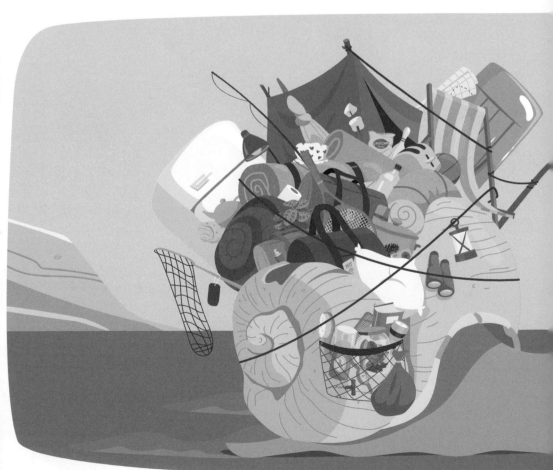

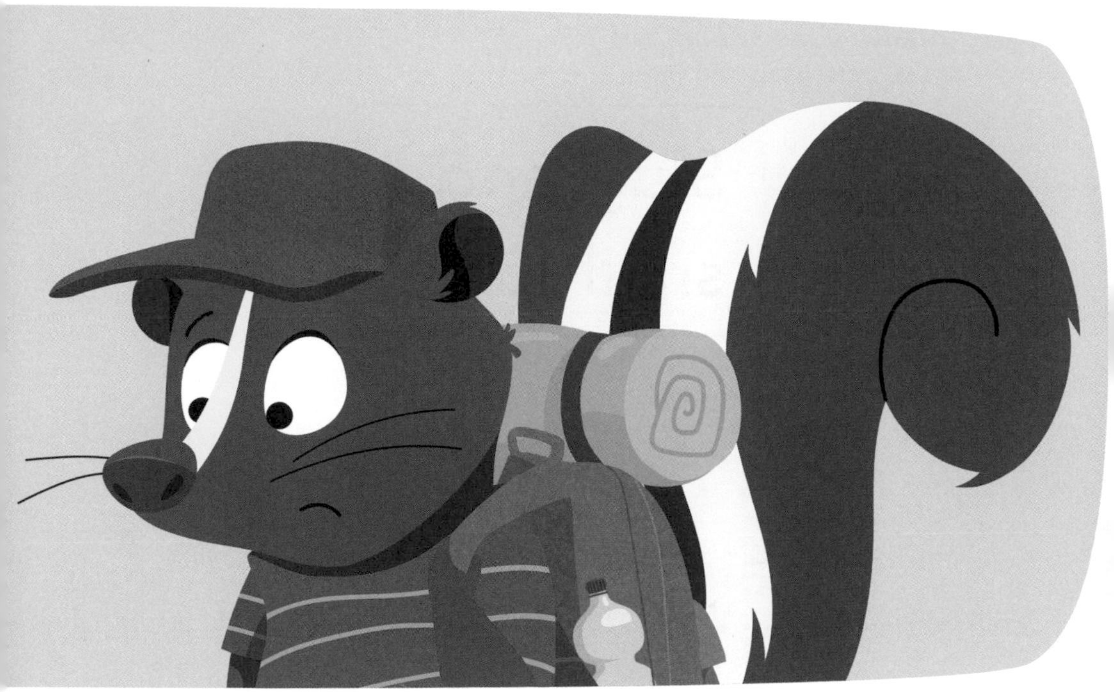

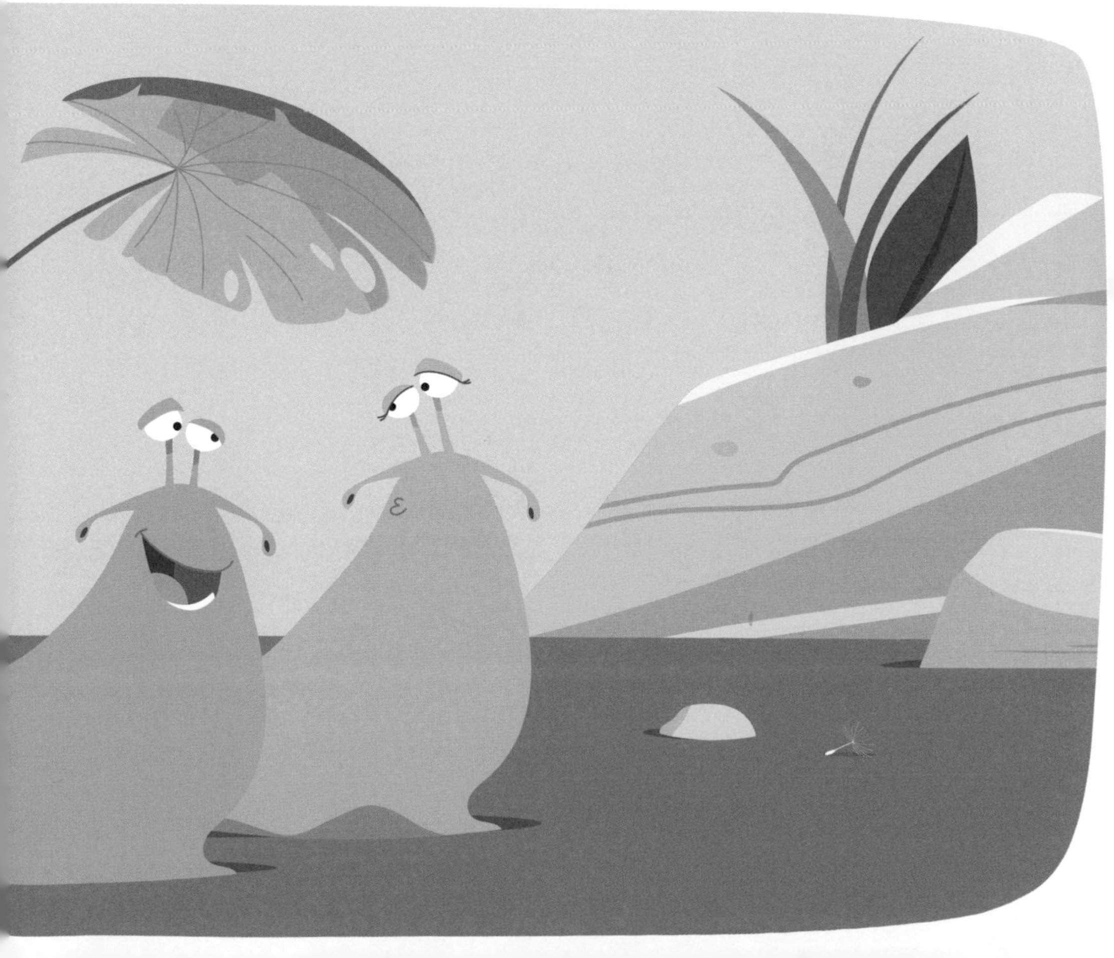

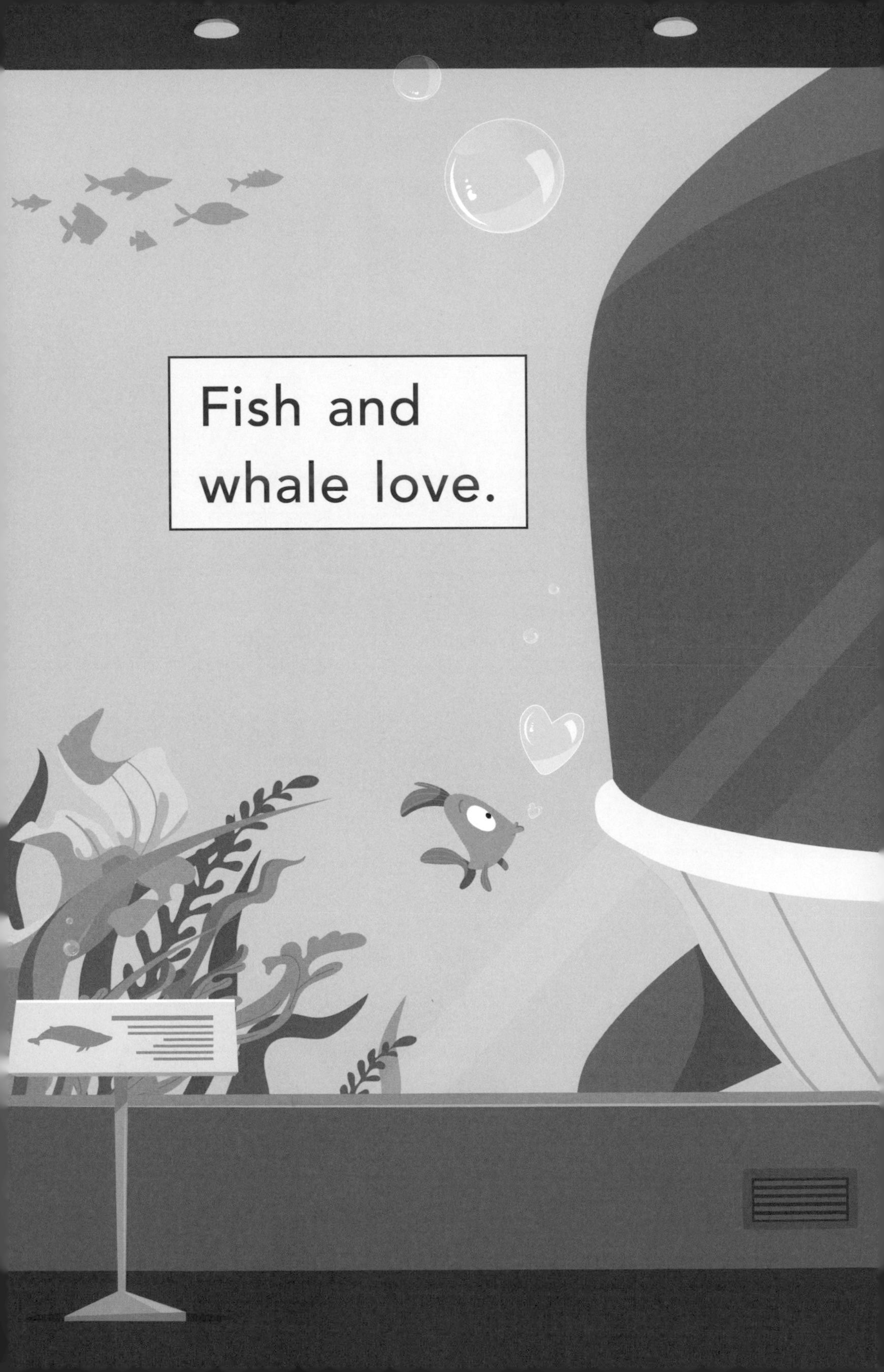

Fish and
whale love.

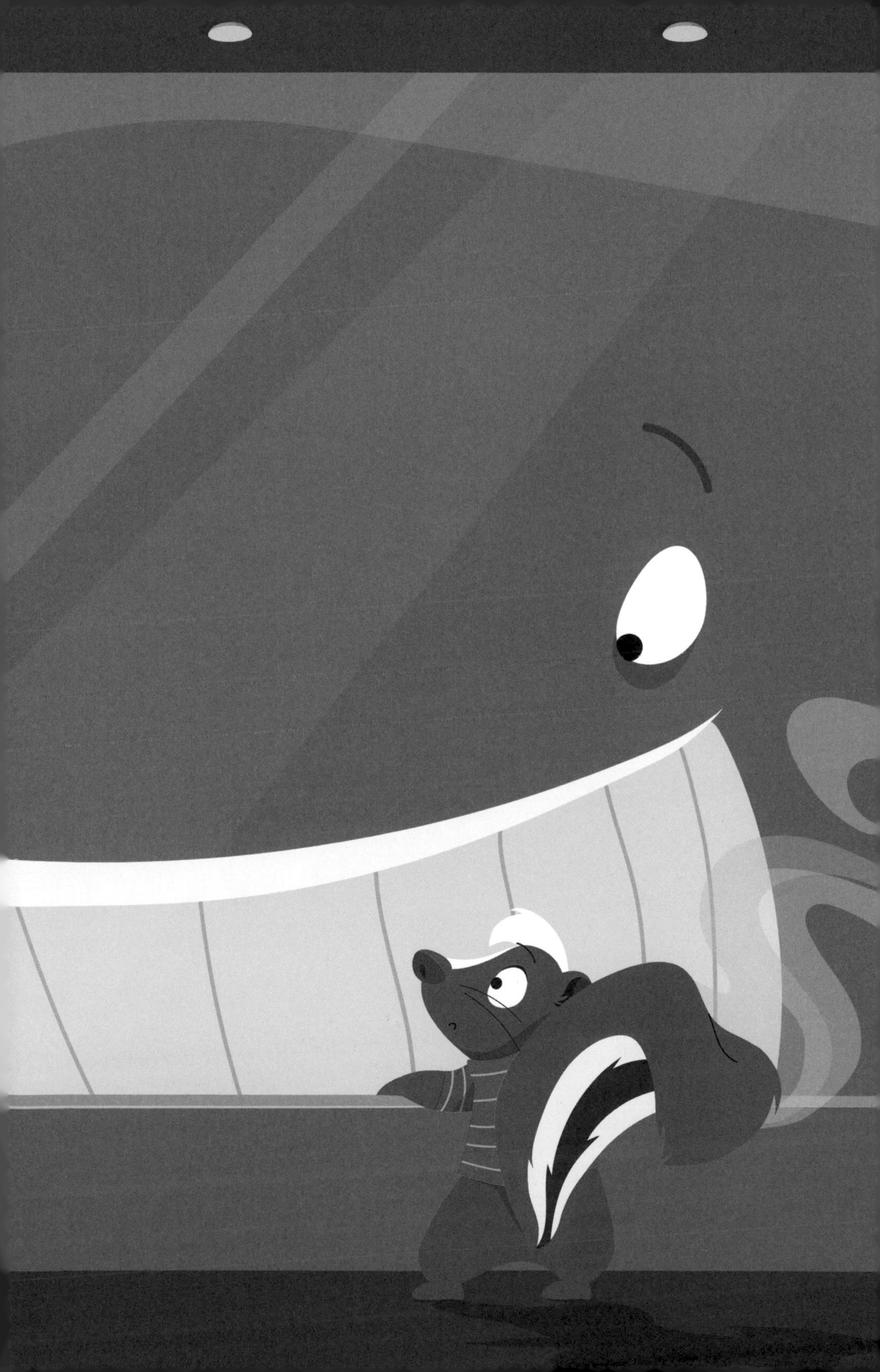

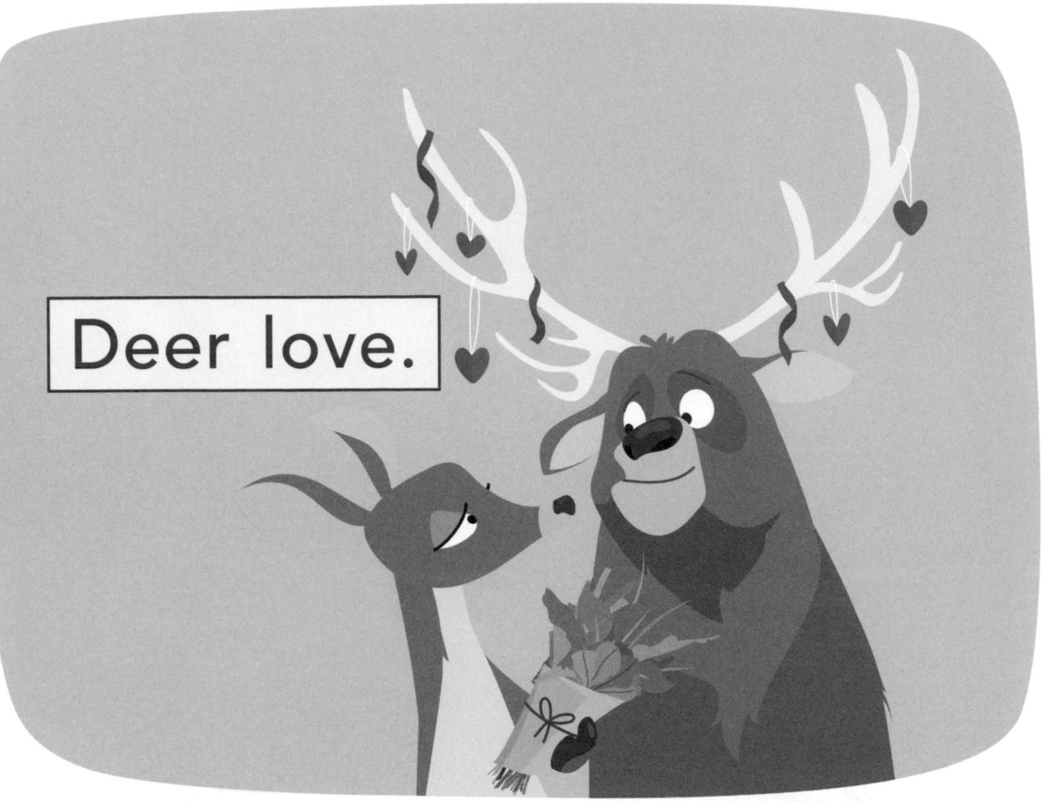
Deer love.

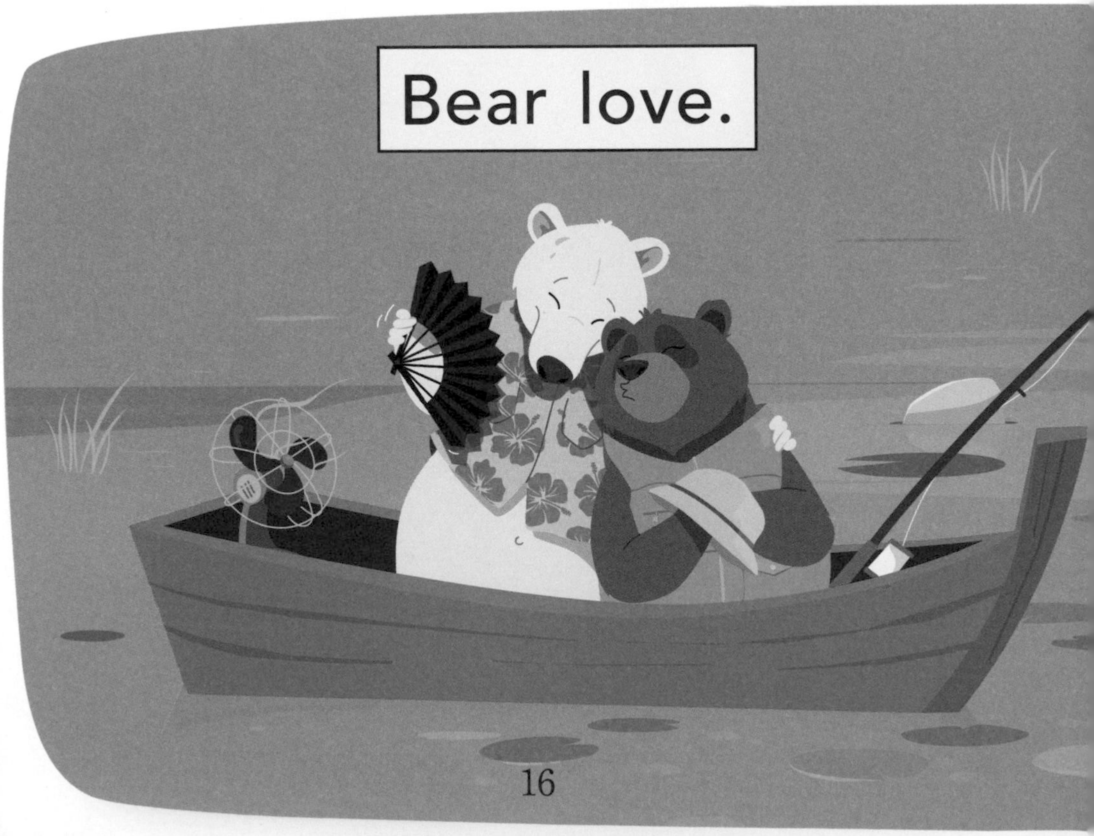
Bear love.

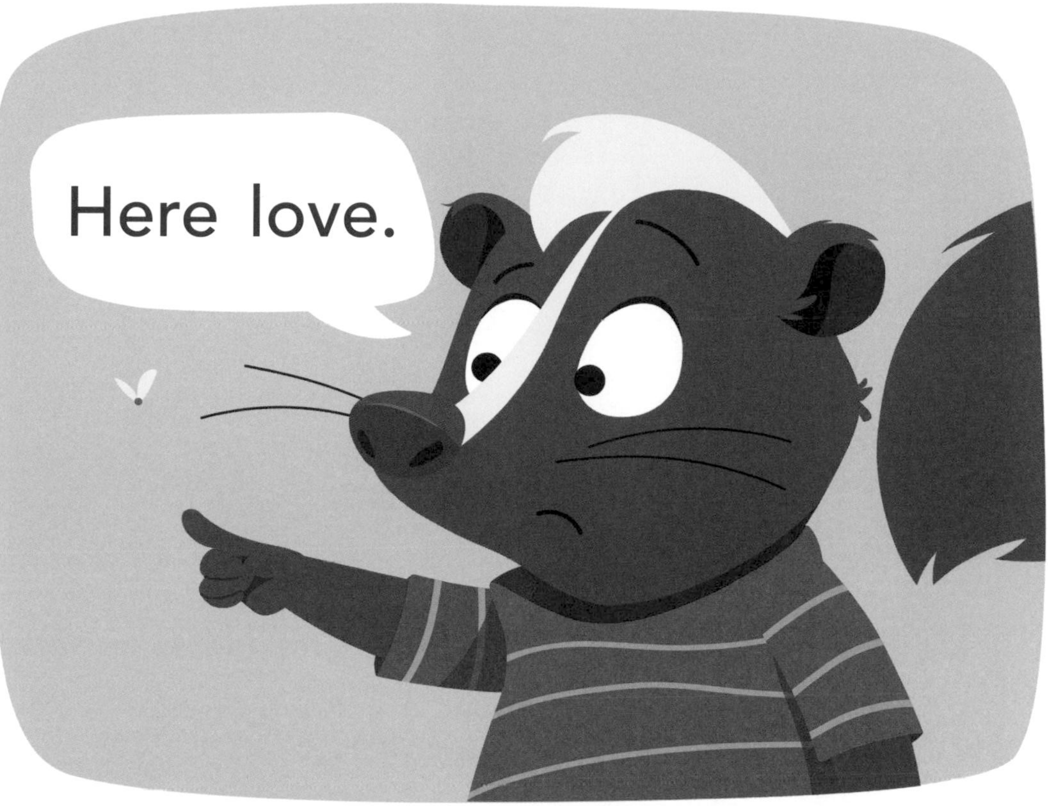
Here love.

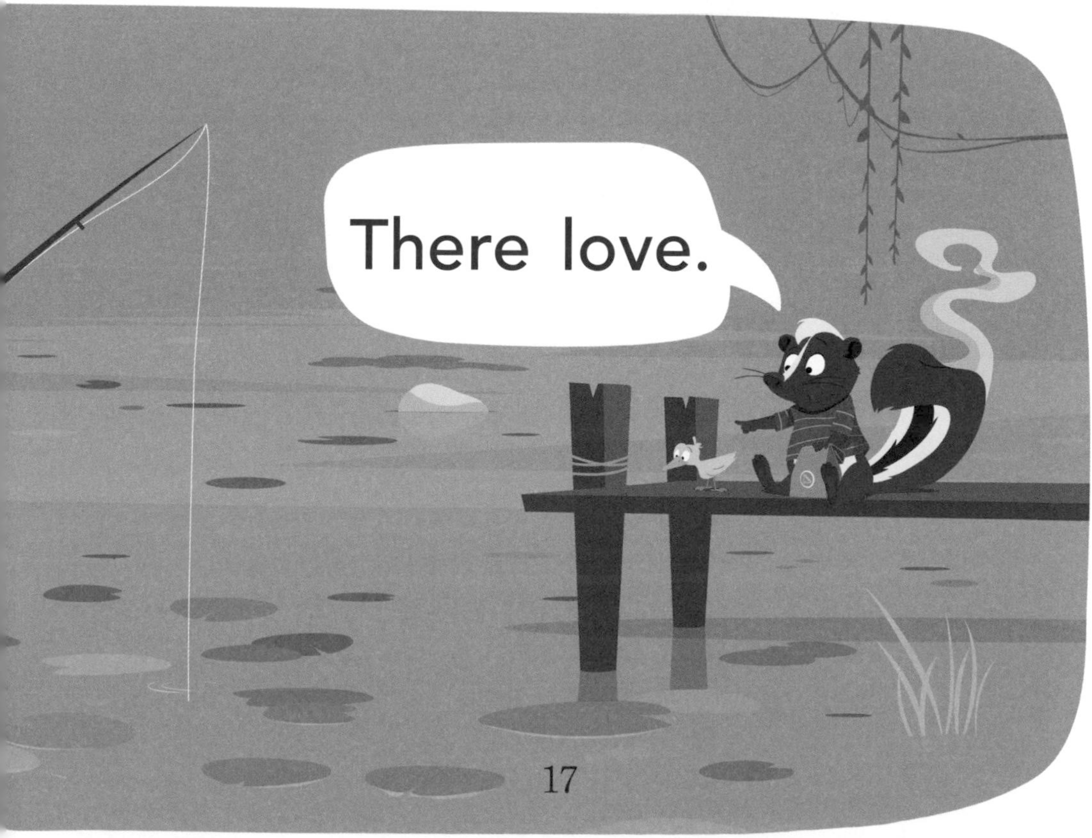
There love.

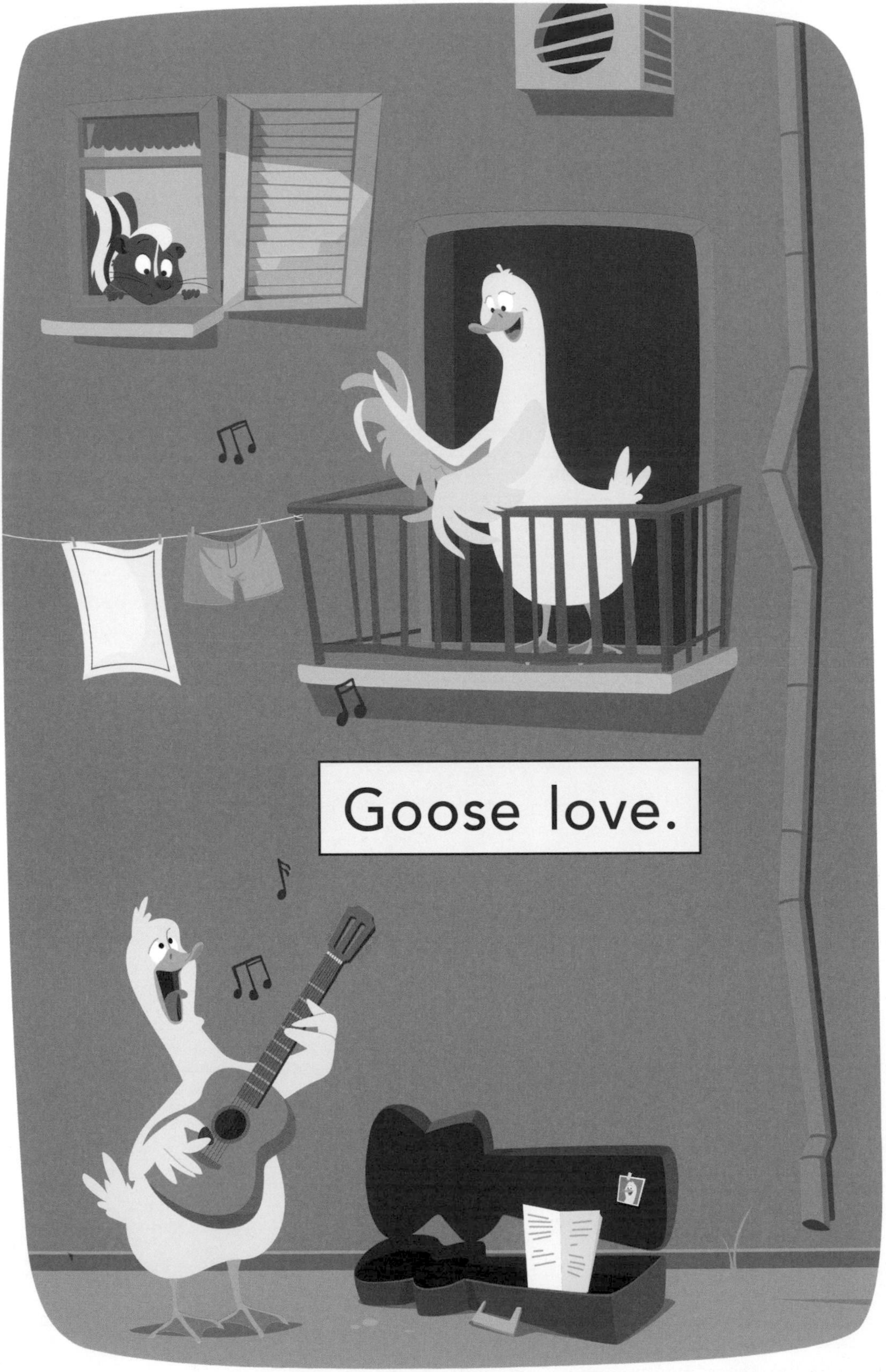

Goose love.

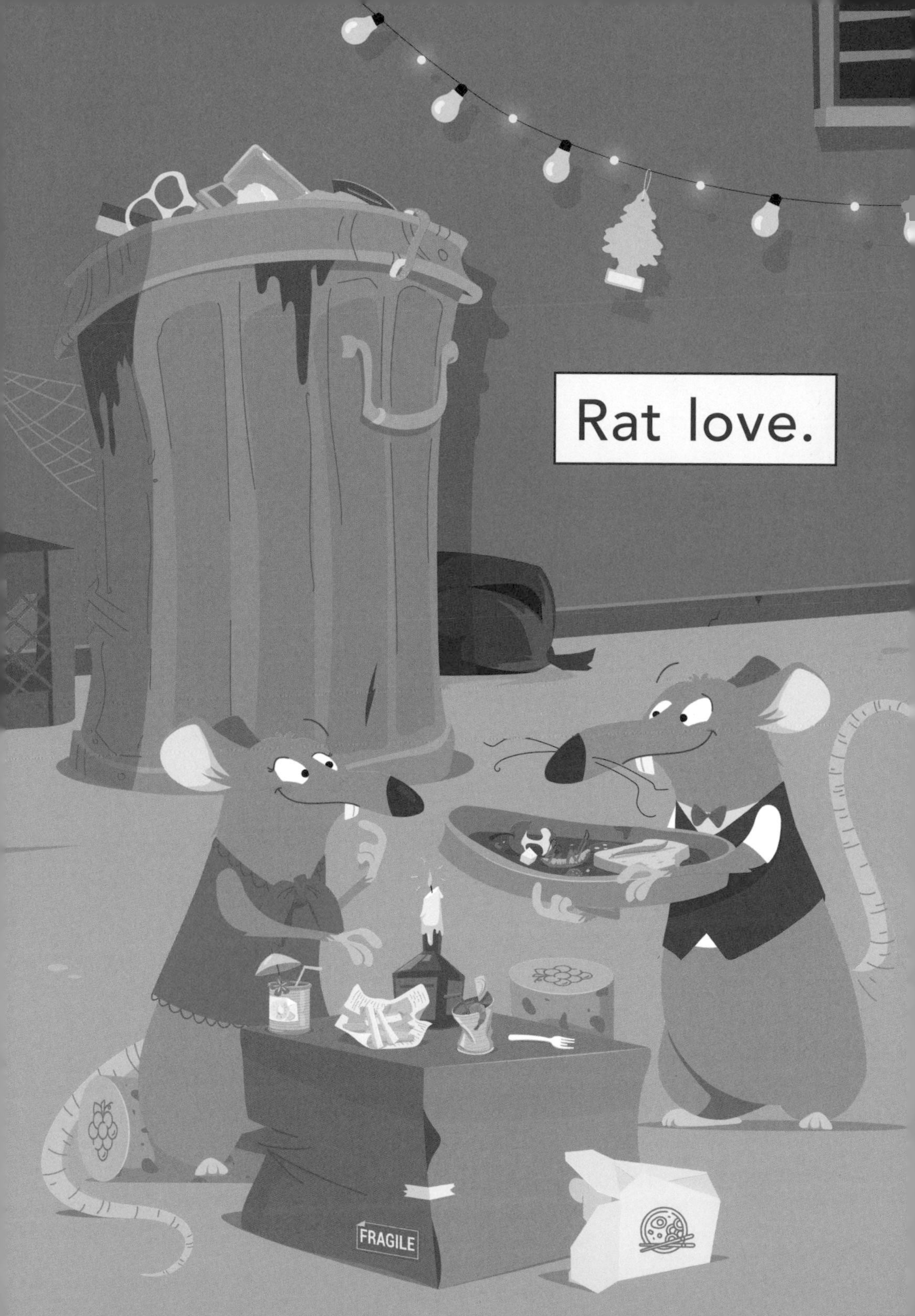
FRAGILE

Rat love.

Moose love.

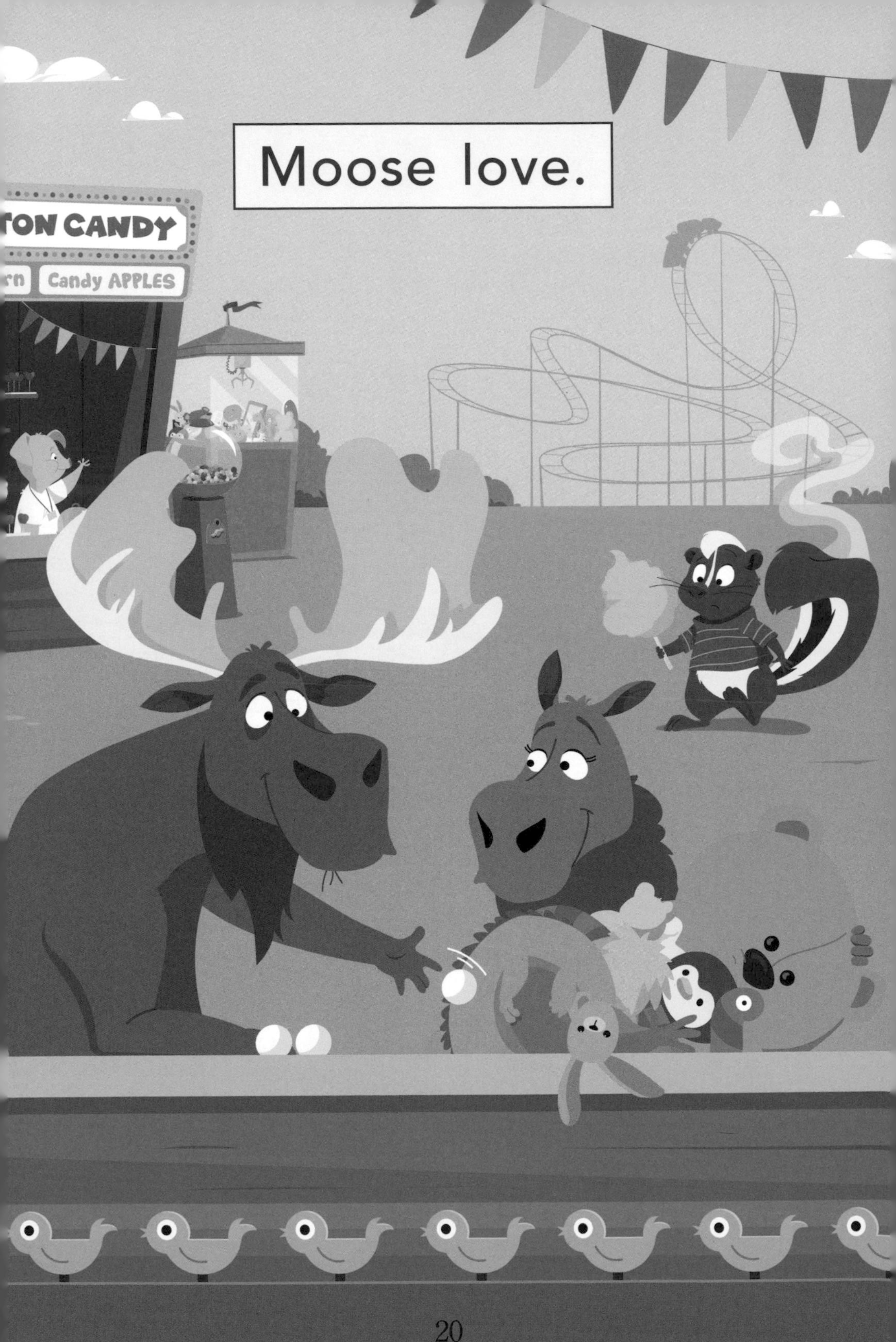
TON CANDY
rn
Candy APPLES

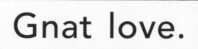
Gnat love.

Old love.

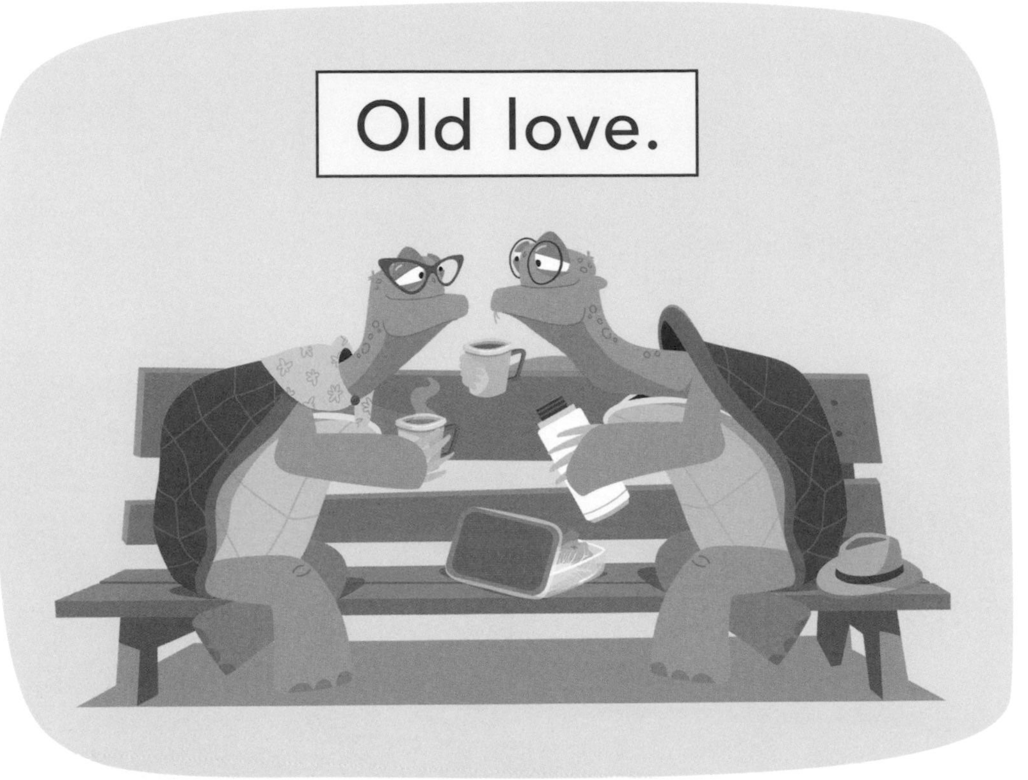

New love.

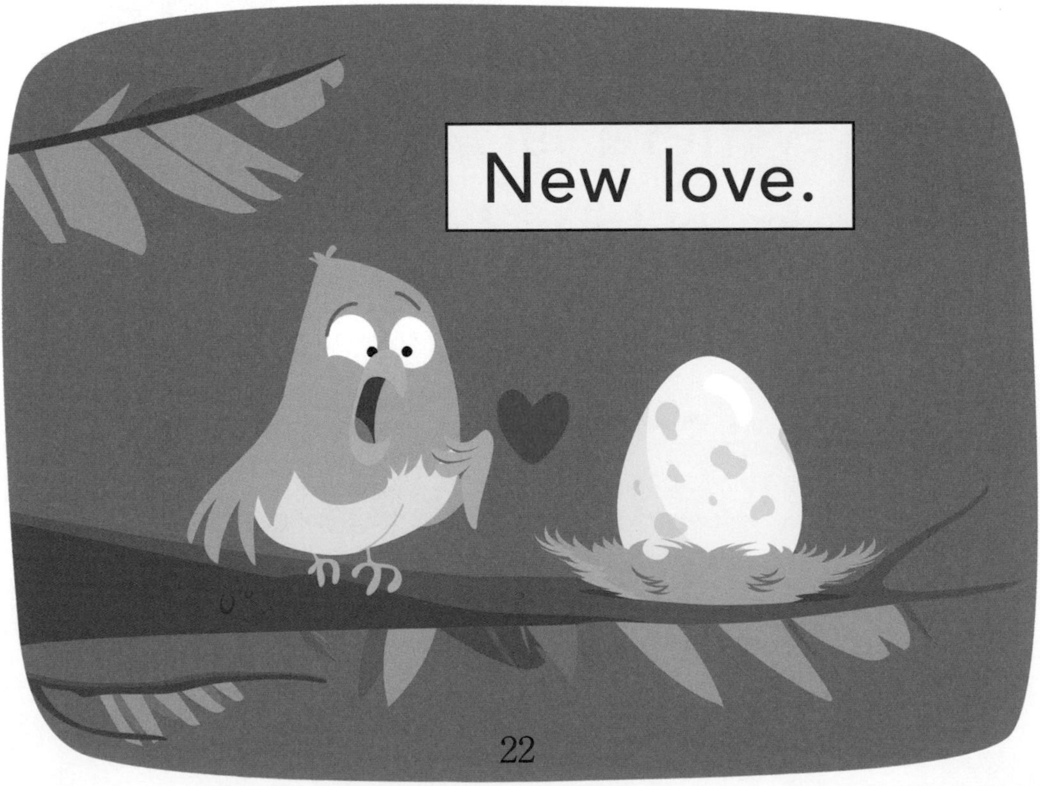

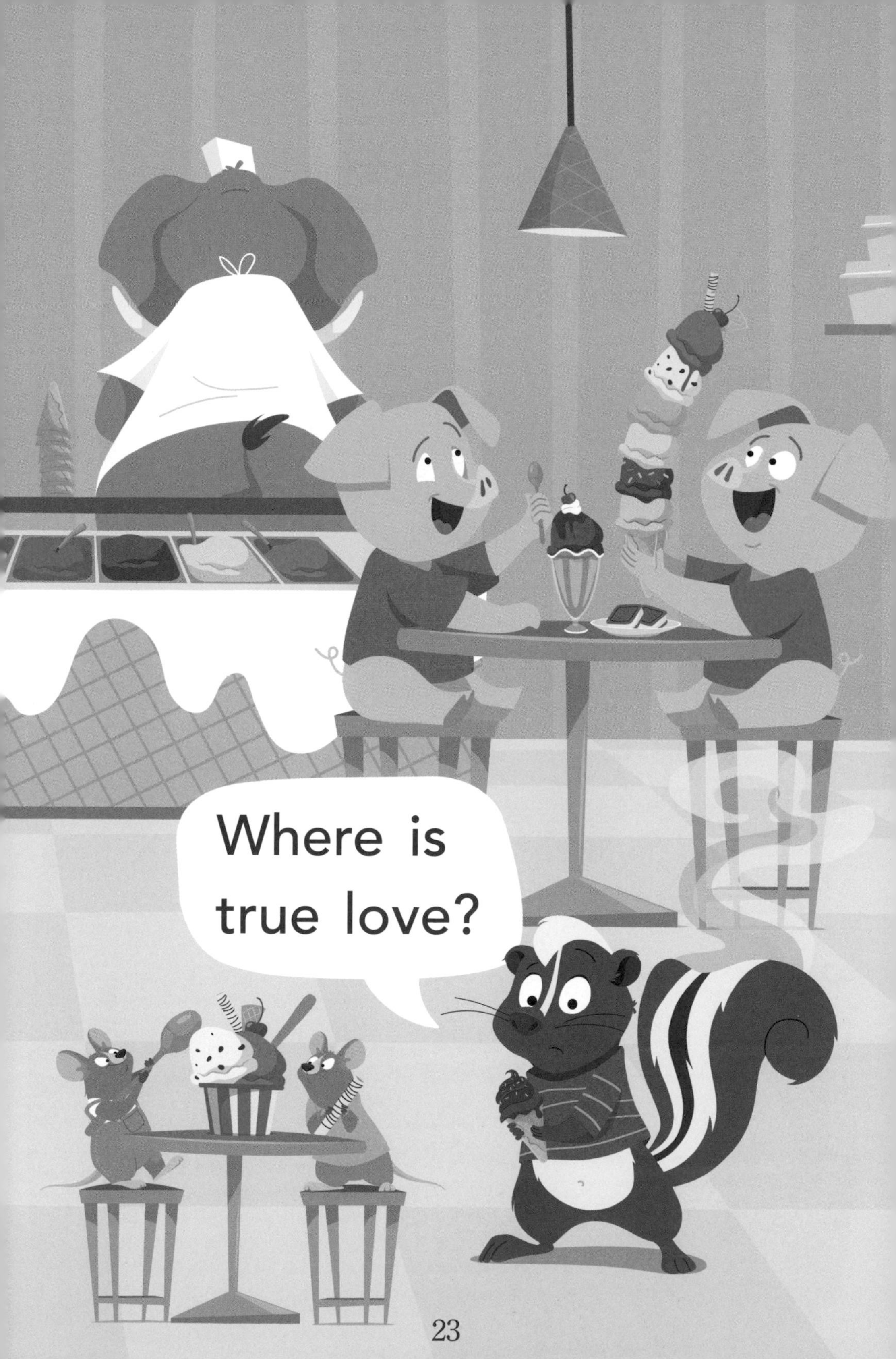
Where is true love?

Eel love.

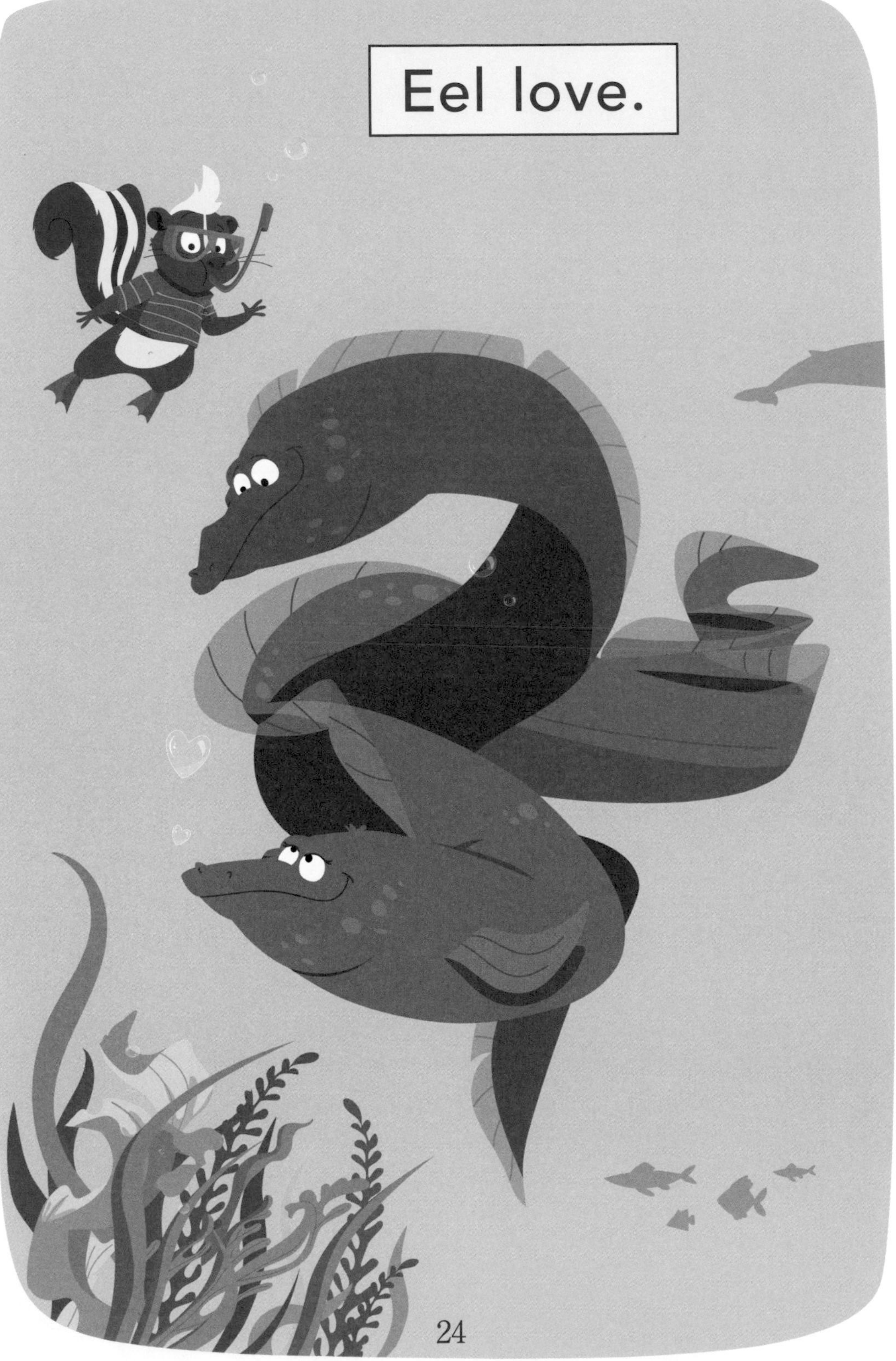

Bee love.

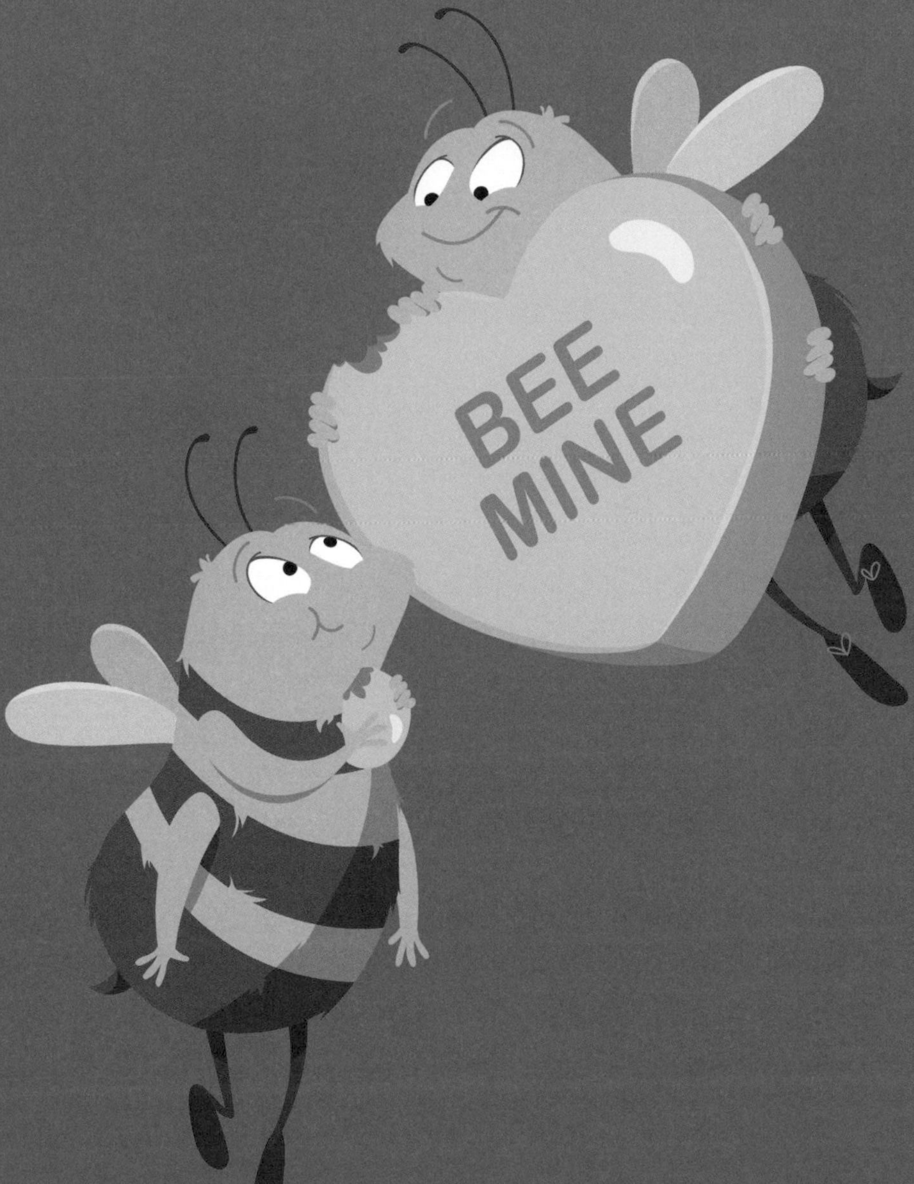
BEE
MINE

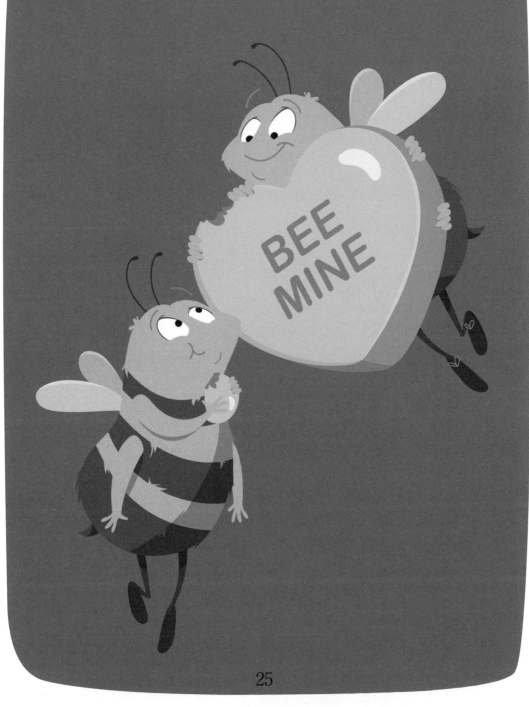

Seal love.

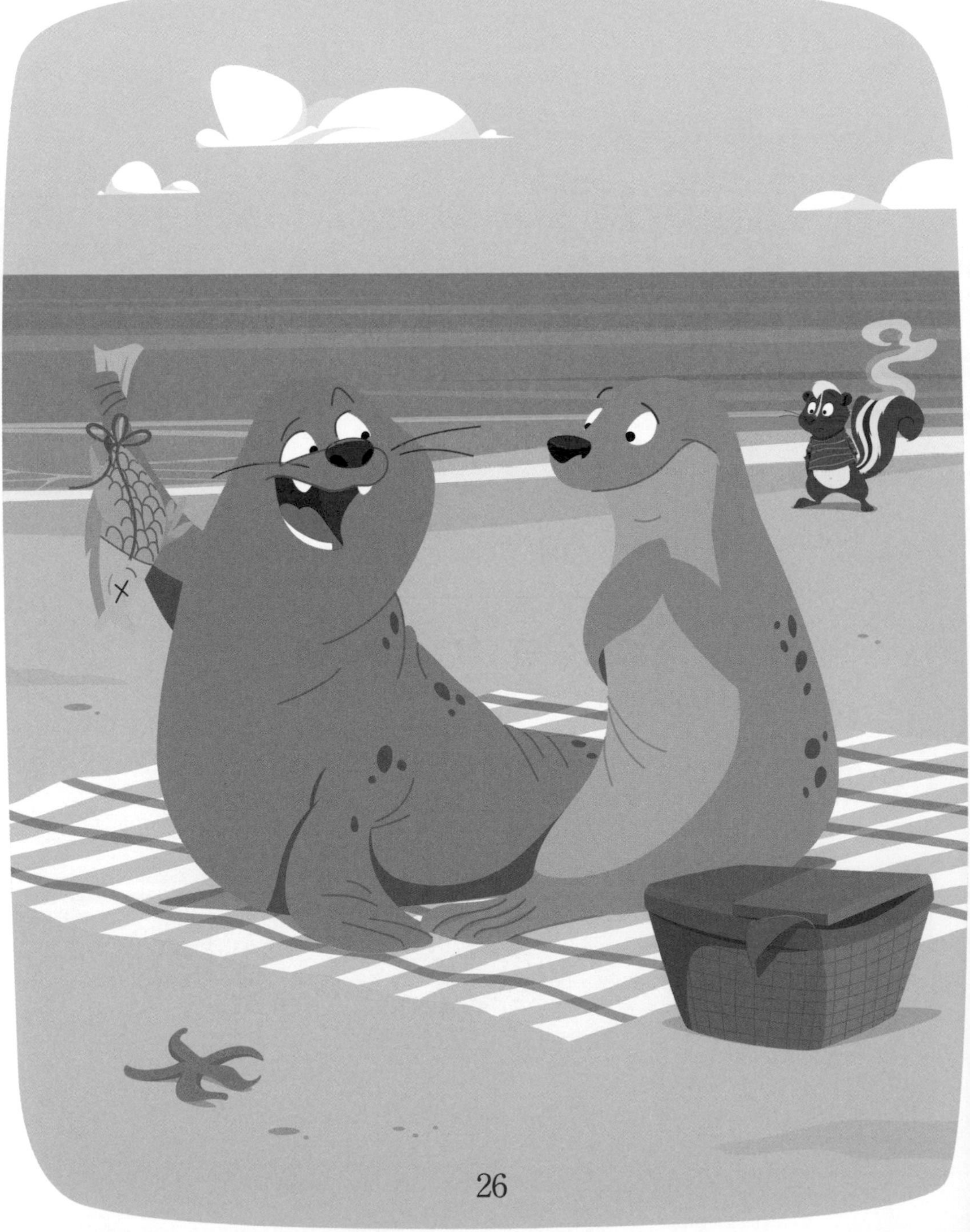

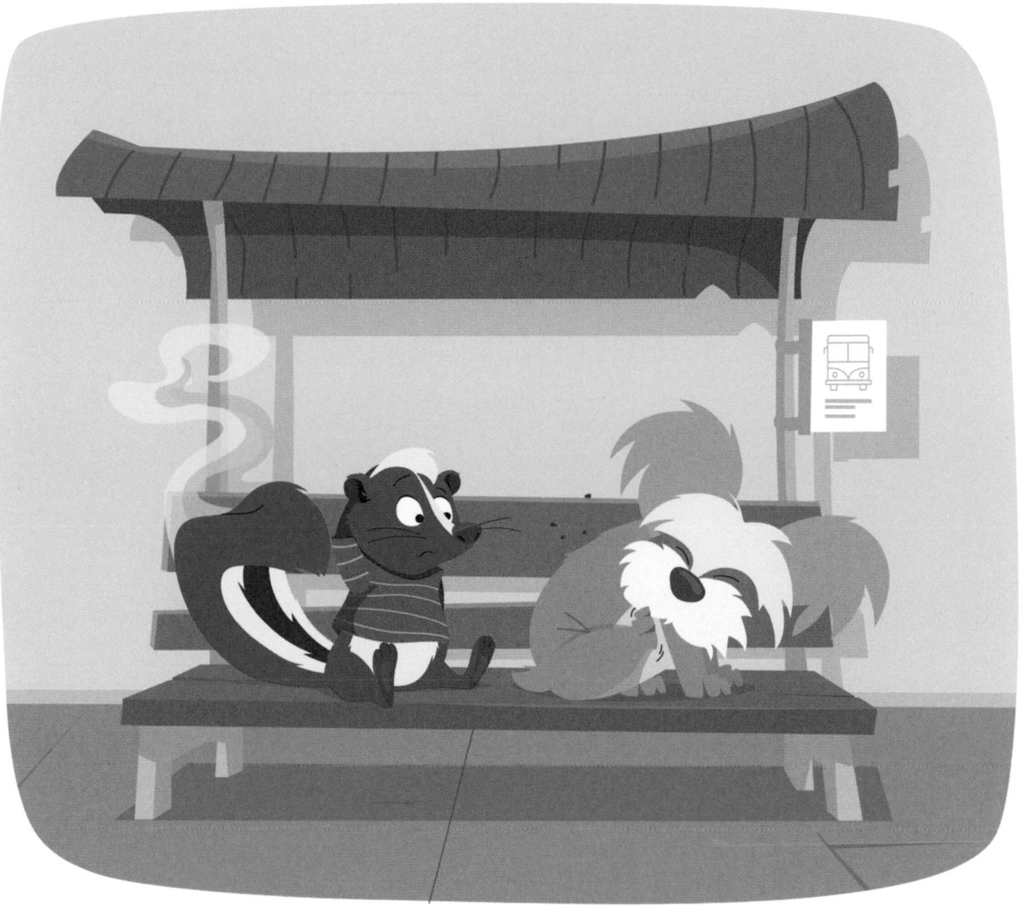

Flea love.

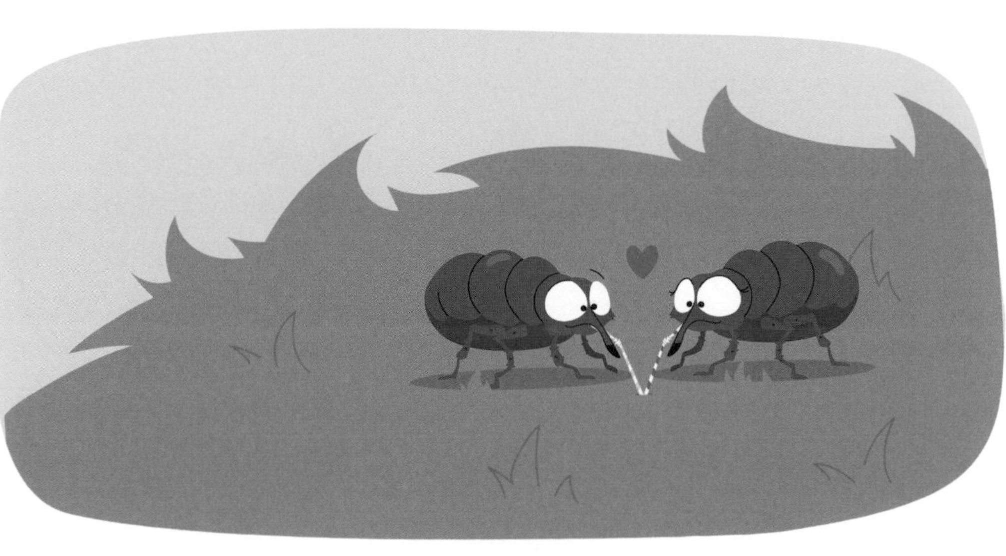

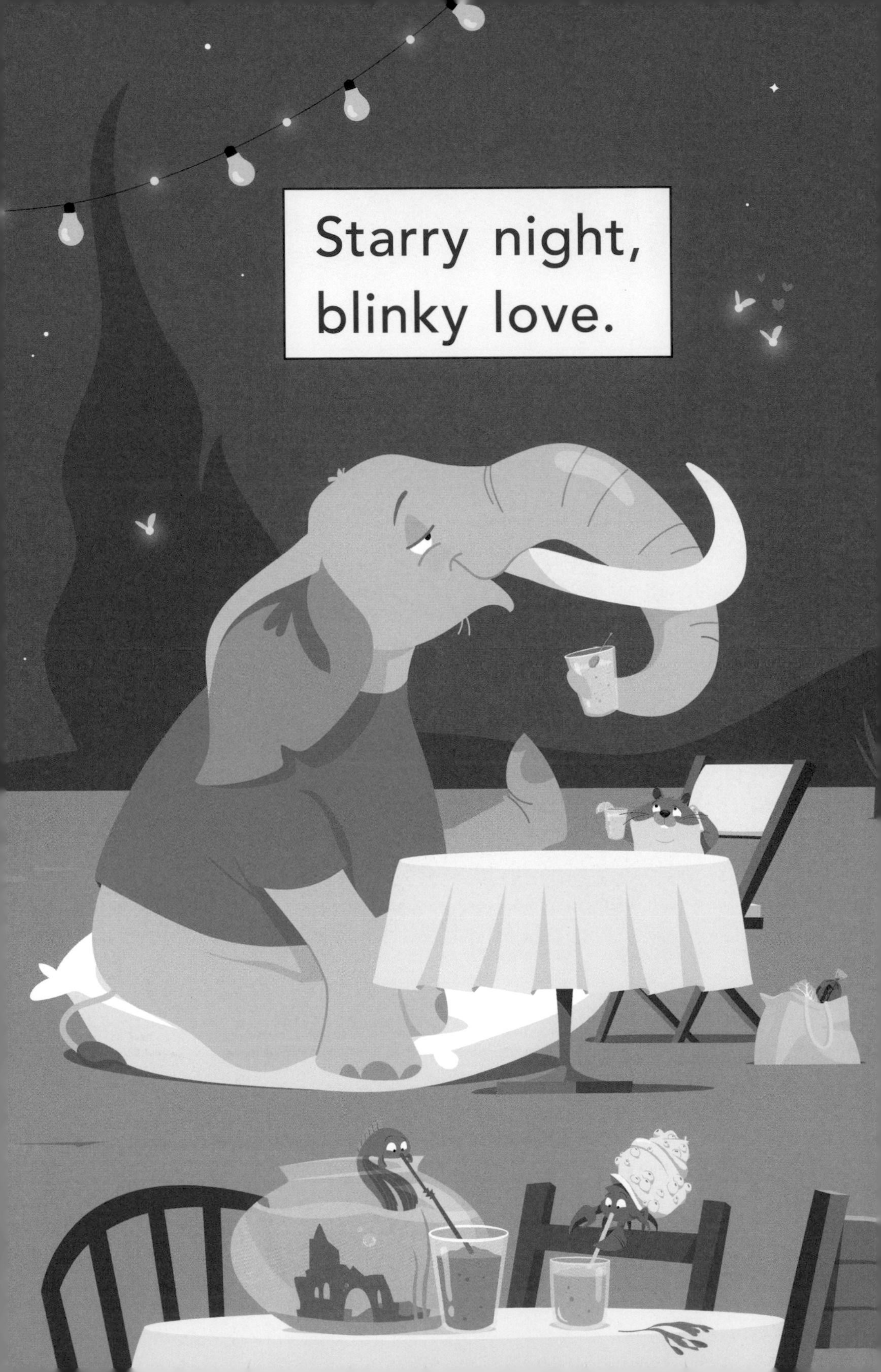
Starry night,
blinky love.

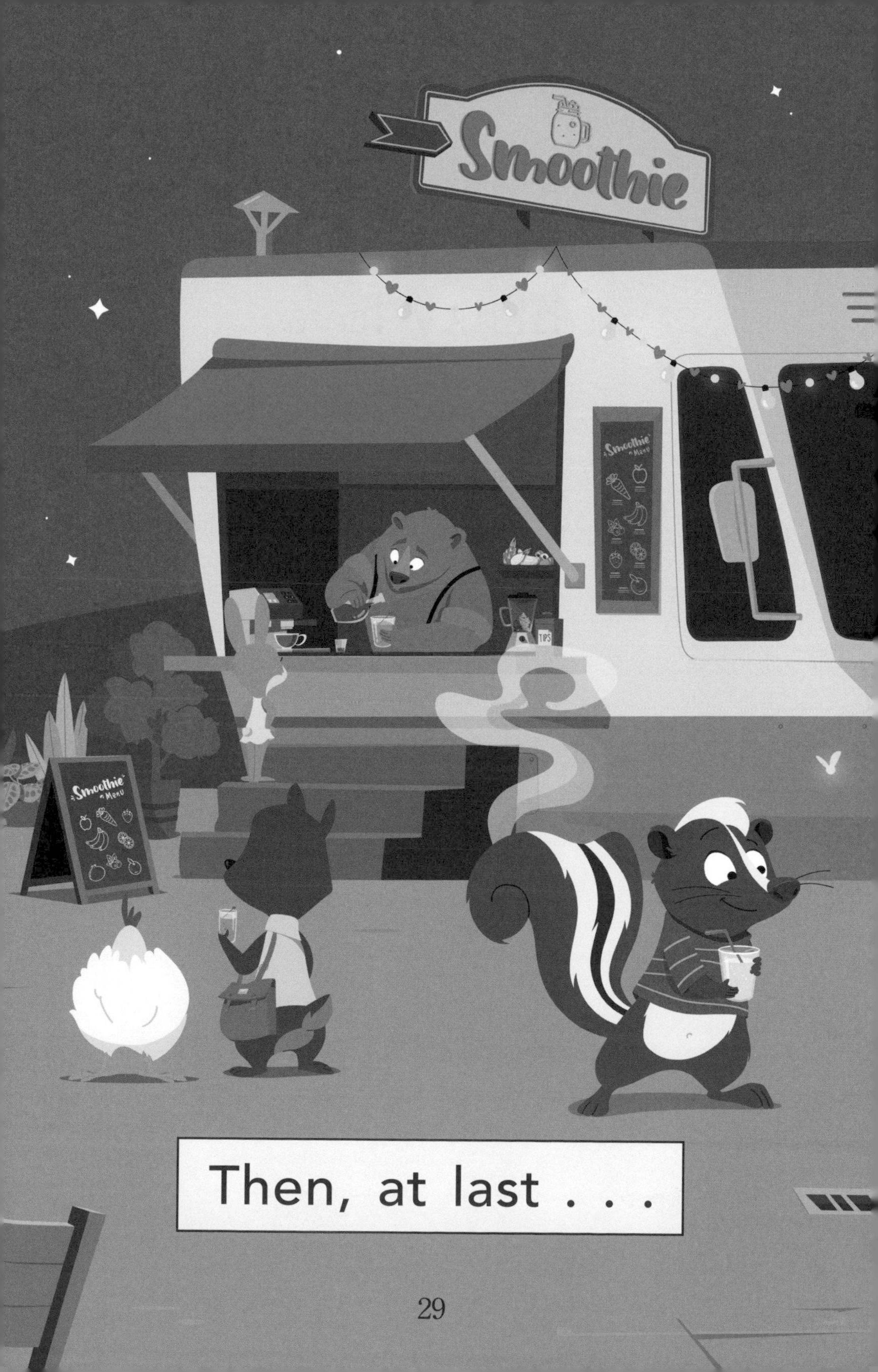
Smoothie
Smoothie Menu
TIPS
Smoothie Menu

Then, at last . . .

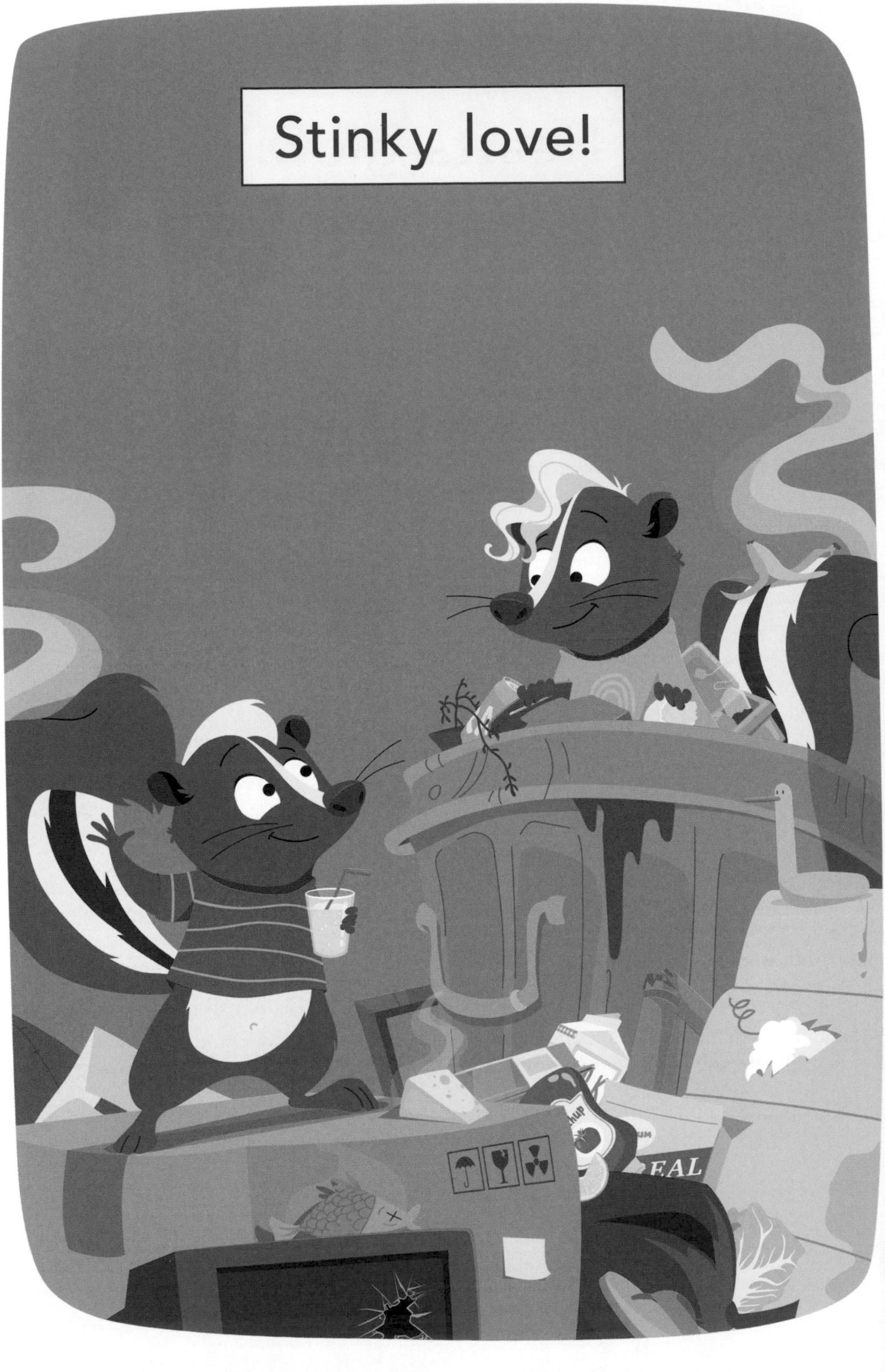
Stinky love!
EAL

Hearts glow.
Eyes shine.

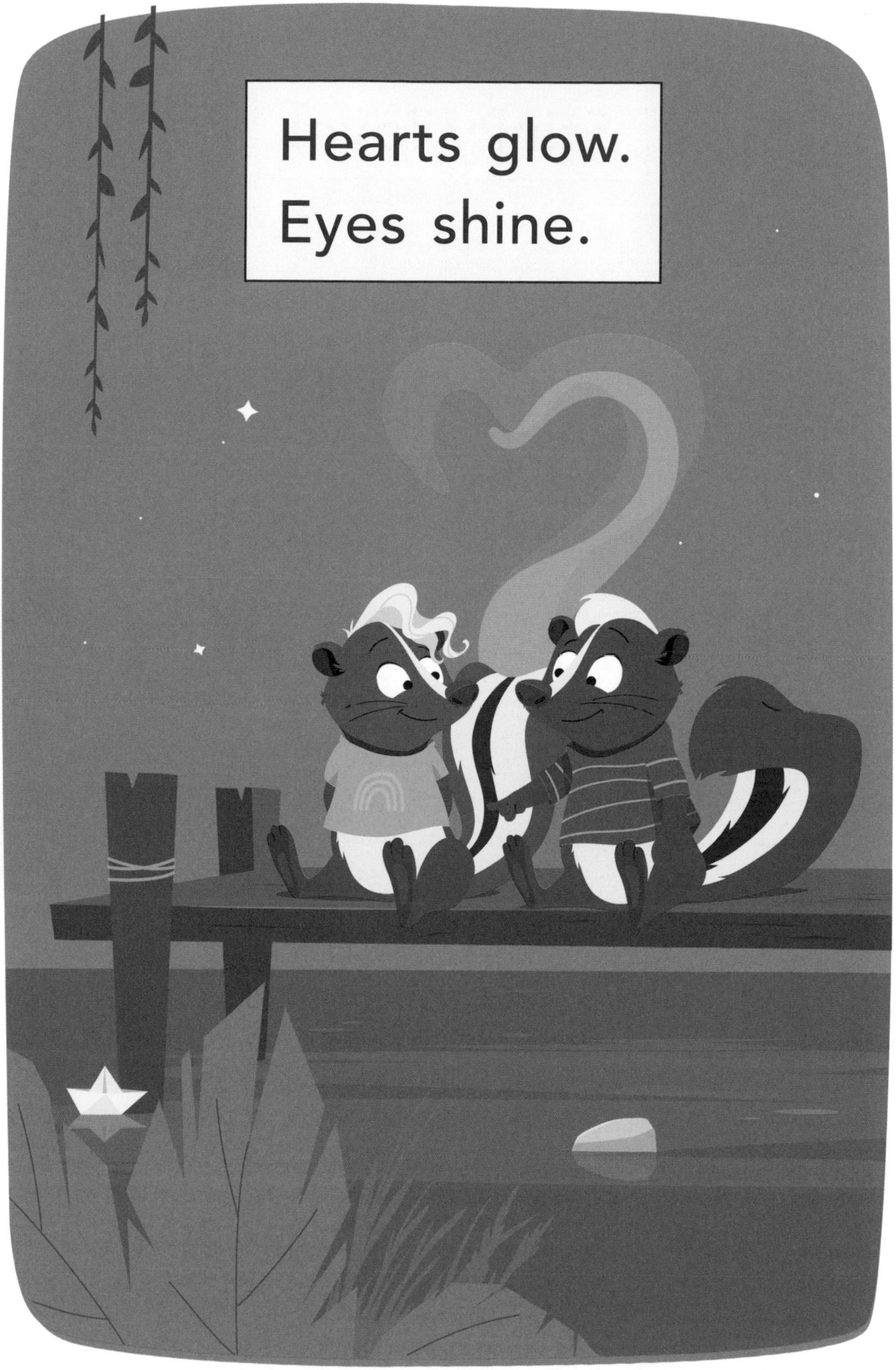

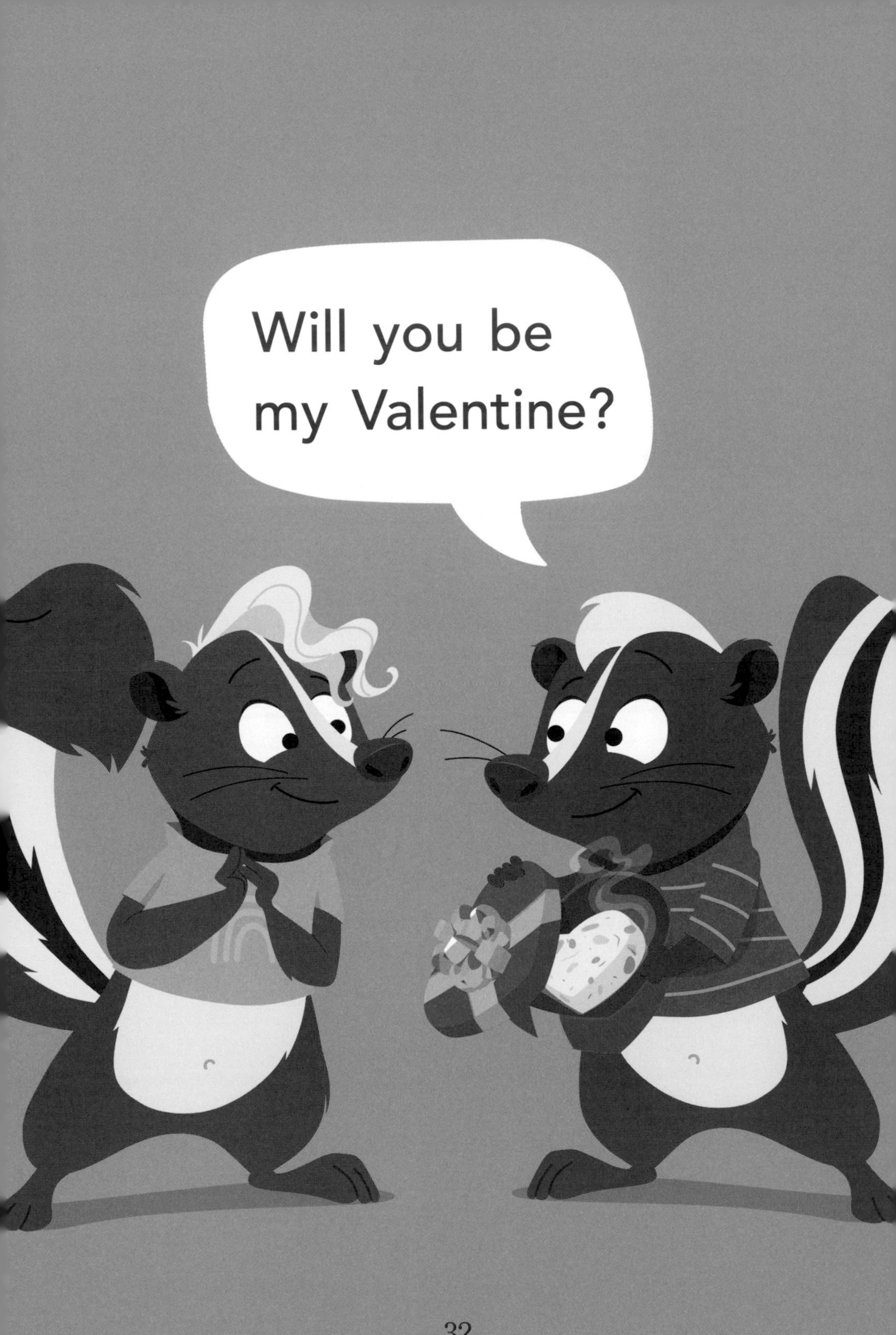
Will you be my Valentine?